FAMILY OF BLUE

THE WEIGHT OF THE BADGE
BOOK 1

KAYLEE ROSE

D0967975

Red's Bookshelf Publishing

Family of Blue: The Weight of the Badge – Book One

www.authorkayleerose.com

Publisher's Note: This is a work of fiction. Names, characters, places, and incidents are a product of the author's imagination. Locales and public names are sometimes used for atmospheric purposes. Any resemblance to actual people, living or dead, or to businesses, companies, events, institutions, or locales is completely coincidental.

Ordering Information:

Quantity sales. Special discounts are available on quantity purchases by corporations, associations, and others. For details, contact the "Special Sales Department" at the address above.

Kaylee Rose – 1st Ed.

He's not just a man in uniform.

He's my hero, my best friend, and the love of my life.

He's my husband.

To the men and women in the first responder family:

Thank you for protecting and caring for our communities.

Please don't forget to take care of yourselves, too.

Come home safe.

1

LANCE

After seven months of intense hands-on training and classwork, I'm finally graduating at the top of my police academy class. Today I will finally become a sworn law enforcement officer, accepting all the responsibilities that come with the job. Tomorrow will be my first day with the Springhill County Sheriff's Department. I'm excited and nervous because it will enable me to apply practical training to real-life situations.

Throughout lunch, my parents are quiet, asking vague questions, avoiding the elephant in the room. I only have a few hours before I need to leave and get ready for my graduation ceremony.

Dad stands and carries our dishes to the kitchen, giving me a moment to speak with Mom alone. Unable to waste any more time skirting around the subject of my career choice, I try to reason with her one last time. With or without her support, the badge will be pinned on my chest. I will wear it with pride.

While facing my mother, I reach across the dining table and hold both of her hands in mine. Before I can say a word, her chest heaves with sobs, breaking my heart. Seeing the fear and sadness in her eyes gives me pause but doesn't change anything. "Mom, please listen to me. I don't want to hurt you, but this is my choice to make. I've always wanted the honor of wearing a badge just like Dad. I want to make both of you proud."

Her first, desperate pleas for me to switch career path fell on deaf ears and nothing has changed since. She was inconsolable the day I joined the academy. I tried to prepare her, dropping hints for months, hoping she'd pick up on them, but denial kept her from seeing the truth. Dad knew about my plans and tried talking to Mom, but she wouldn't hear of it.

"We are proud of you, Lance, but why can't you choose something else? A job where I don't have to worry about getting a knock on the door telling me my son is hurt or, worse, dead. When your dad retired, I thought my nights of pacing the floors, drifting in and out of a restless sleep were over, and now, it will start all over again."

"I know telling you not to worry won't help ease your mind. It's what moms do."

My mother tears up again. "Don't you remember how hard it was while you were young? I felt like a single mother most of the time. Do you really want that when you have a family of your own?" She's grasping at straws, trying to find anything she thinks will make me change my mind.

I hear her words and everything she says is the truth, but the force is important to me. The days when Dad would miss my games due to work filled me with anger and resentment. It seemed work always came before Mom and me. Those memories almost kept me from even considering joining the force.

When asked the dreaded *what do you want to do with the rest of your life* question that plagues every young adult, I began researching what might interest me. Looking at my choices, I kept going back to law enforcement and added it to

2

my shortlist of options. It wasn't until I spent an evening with my dad and his partner on the job that my decision was solidified. Watching him interact with his partners and the public gave me a whole new level of respect for officers. Especially the man who came home to Mom and me every night.

With his simple announcement of *I'm home,* I could see the tension lift from my mom's shoulders. The relief she felt when Dad walked through the door was obvious to me even as a young boy.

Dad would continue down the hallway into his bedroom and begin the process of changing from Officer Malloy into what I now think of as the man behind the badge. On autopilot, he'd remove his gun belt, place his weapon in the safe, change out of his crisp blue uniform and seek out my mom, who was most likely in the kitchen getting ready to serve dinner. With a flourish worthy of an old romance movie, Dad would kiss her and whisper how much he missed and loved her. Every night the same thing. I think the routine gave us all a sense of comfort and control over the things we never wanted to imagine could happen while Dad was on the job.

I release my mother's hands before reaching into my back pocket for one of Dad's monogramed handkerchiefs. Gently, I place it in her hand, closing her fingers around the thin cloth. I always carry one with me. Mom buys him a new box each Christmas. By December they all seemed to disappear. He had a habit of giving them to anyone who needed it to dry their tears. When Dad retired, the tradition was passed on to me making me think Mom knew this day was coming.

Mom doesn't look up. Her eyes are fixated on my larger hand enveloping hers. When her trembling hands relax, I stand, lean down and kiss her tear stained cheek. "I'm sorry, Mom, but I have to do this for me. I hope you'll be at my graduation and pin the badge to my uniform, but I understand if you can't come. I love you."

With each step I take, my boots feel as if they are full of

cement. I fight the urge to walk back to my mother, for one last hug, but I know it's only delaying the inevitable, making it harder for both of us. I have no doubt that deep down in her soul she understands why I must do this.

Dad meets me at the front door. A plain blue t-shirt and faded jeans are his daily uniform now. He still looks like a cop, only his hair isn't cut as short as it used to be.

"Stay home with Mom instead of coming to the ceremony. It's really not that big a deal." It is a big deal and I want them there more than I let on.

His brow wrinkles with concern. "I'll try to talk to her again. She loves you. Remember what I told you. As hard as it is to be an officer, it's even harder to be the one at home wait-ing. For an officer to handle the emotions and stress of the job, the weight of the badge must be carried by the entire family. It wasn't easy when I wore my badge and it will be even harder for her to see you wearing yours. She'll get there though. She's prouder of you than you'll ever know. We both are." He pulls me into a strong bear hug like he used to when I was a kid.

"I won't forget. I love you, Dad." The mix of emotions I feel keep me from saying anything more.

Before opening the door to exit, I pause to look inside the curio cabinet and stare at the memory box displaying Dad's badge and patches.

Filling my dad's shoes won't be easy, but I promise to work hard every day to make him proud.

2

KELLIE

After two days of non-stop calling, texting, and emailing my drug addicted sister, Leslie, and without a response, I decide to visit her in person. Instinct tells me something is terribly wrong.

The constant ringing sound through my car speakers infuriates me. I hit the steering wheel with my palms and shout out my anger as if it will cause her to miraculously hear me and pick up. "Damn it, Leslie, where the fuck are you? Answer your phone."

Just like the last time I called her voicemail picks up. Leslie's sweet and innocent greeting betrays the reality of the lifestyle she leads. "Hey, it's Leslie. You know what to do. I'll call you back soon."

"Where are you? I'm sick of waiting for you to return my call. I'm on my way to your apartment now and you better be there. We need to talk about Rory. I want to see her now. I'll be there in less than five minutes." I disconnect the call and scream, letting out some of the rage which has been building up inside me for months.

I've reached my breaking point. Finally deciding I won't wait another day to remove my two-year-old niece, Rory, from the unhealthy and dangerous environment they live in. I drive faster than I should, trying to reach the other side of town while it's still daylight. The court may not approve, but I don't care.

As I drive through this rundown neighborhood, I see evidence of widespread neglect. It's unfortunate how this once family friendly area became overrun by drug dealers, addicts, and other types of criminals. The sadness I feel about the state of this town won't distract me from seeing Rory.

I tear into the parking lot, not caring about the red, no parking zone.

Fuck it! They can tow my car as long as I reach Rory before my sister does something I can't fix.

Taking the stairs two at a time I reach her apartment and pound on the rotting, old, wooden door. When nobody answers, I kick the door, breaking the frame too easily.

The living room in this tiny one-bedroom apartment is so cluttered with junk and boxes, the carpet is no longer visible. It makes me wonder if Rory is ever taken out of her crib with such little room to roam. Then again, it's probably better she doesn't crawl around in this filthy hovel.

A small loveseat sits beside the doorway under a window. So much dirt is built up sunlight is barely visible through the panes of glass. My sister and some guy I've never seen before are sprawled out beside each other. I storm across the room to Leslie, rage burning inside of me. "Leslie! Wake up!" I try to rouse her from whatever drug induced sleep she is in. "Can't you hear Rory crying for you?"

Her head rolls towards me and she mumbles something I can't understand. She's so strung out she can barely speak let alone take care of her daughter.

My inspection of Leslie stops as I hear Rory's increasingly desperate cries. I step over the boxes and continue in the direction of my niece's heartbreaking sobs.

As I walk past the kitchenette, the stench from the sink-full of dishes and bags of garbage hit me full on, causing me to retch violently. I swallow the bile down, pulling my T-shirt up over my nose and mouth to continue my search.

Inside the cluttered bedroom, I find Rory in her crib, standing on tiptoes, violently shaking the rails and screaming hoarsely for her momma. As I get closer, she backs away into the corner of her crib, dragging a raggedy blanket with her. My heart plummets when I see the horrific state she's in. Her eyes are red and swollen, and snot covers her face. The pink onesie pajamas she has on are too small. I doubt she's been changed in days.

"I'm here baby. I've got you. Come to Aunt Kellie." In two big steps she reaches out to me, almost diving into my arms. I lift her out of the crib and cradle her against my chest, peppering the top of her head with kisses while my body naturally sways side to side. "I'm so sorry I didn't get here sooner."

Still clutching Rory tight, I walk back into the main room to tell Leslie I'm taking Rory with me.

"Leslie. Can you hear me? Leslie?" Shifting Rory to my hip, I try to wake my sister by shaking her shoulder and notice her eyes have rolled to the back of her head. Saliva gurgles from her throat.

Not wanting to set Rory on the floor, I struggle to get my phone out of my back pocket before calling 911 for help. A female dispatcher answers immediately. "911. What's your emergency?"

"I need an ambulance. I think my sister and the guy with her have overdosed."

"Okay, stay on the line until the ambulance arrives."

I give the dispatcher the address and begin answering her questions. "Are they breathing?"

I can see the rise and fall of his chest and hear the wet rattling sound escaping Leslie's throat on each exhale. I check for a pulse, placing my fingers alongside her neck. The faint beat under my fingertips gives me a sliver of hope she will survive. "Yes, they are, but my sister looks really bad. I can barely feel her pulse and it sounds like she's choking."

"They're breathing, that's good. Now are you able to place your sister on a flat surface and turn her on her side?"

"Yeah, hold on." To free up my hands, I place my phone on speaker and set it on the edge of the couch. After kicking some boxes out of my way, and with Rory balanced on my hip, I pull Leslie's limp body off the loveseat to the floor. I speak loudly so the dispatcher can hear me. "Okay, she's on the floor."

"Good, now turn her on her side. This will help in case she vomits, stopping her from aspirating on the bile."

I awkwardly kneel beside Leslie, roll her to her side, and brace her body against my thighs to keep her in position. "Okay. She sounds better. How much longer until they get here?"

"It looks like they're on the scene now." Right then sirens pierce the air announcing the arrival of the ambulance. The faceless voice which has kept me calm tells me she can disconnect the call now that they've arrived. I thank her and shove my phone into my pocket before trying to figure out what to do next.

As angry as I am about this situation, I love my big sister and seeing her self-destruct hurts me more than she would ever realize. "Leslie, please wake up. You and Rory will be fine. I'll get you help, and you can live with me until things get better. Rory needs her mom and I need my sister. Please wake up."

I swipe the hair from Leslie's face, tucking it behind her ear. The drugs have taken their toll on my big sis. Her once flawless complexion has scars and small red marks from the skin ulcers caused by her addiction. Leslie never needed makeup. It only served to cover up her natural beauty that seemed to stun every boy in school. A long-forgotten memory of Leslie trying to teach me how to apply eyeliner and blush comes to mind. I looked like a clown, but she didn't tease me. Instead, she sat me in front of the vanity mirror and taught me how to apply it with a light hand, with just the right amount of color to accentuate what she said was my inner beauty.

Another awful gasping sound fills the room, snapping me out of happier times and back to the sad reality of my sister's drug dependency. Leslie's raspy cough worries me. "Hey, remember that day you taught me how to put on makeup and we ended up eating cake frosting from the can and watching movies all night? I need you here so we can tell Rory all about those funny stories from our past. Come on, sis, just open your eyes."

I hear the loud steps of heavy boots running up the stairs before I see two paramedics walk inside. They weave through the garbage, finding a place to set their equipment before asking me any questions.

"Ma'am. Did you call 911?"

"Yes. My sister and that guy need help." Standing up, I move out of their way, until I feel my back against the wall. I shift Rory in my arms, over to my left shoulder and watch intently, not believing what is playing out in front of me.

"And what about you and the child? Do you need help?" His voice is calm and direct.

"I'm fine and she seems okay. I just got here. Please help my sister." Rory's fingers pull tight on my T-shirt when she snuggles her face into my neck like she's trying to hide.

After pulling their latex gloves on, one paramedic checks the man for a pulse while the other kneels beside Leslie to begin his assessment of her.

"Sir, can you hear me?" The EMT forces the seemingly lifeless man's eyelids open and uses a small pen light to assess pupil diameter. Requiring access to his chest area, the EMT uses scissors to cut his T-shirt up the middle. Using the knuckles on his gloved fist, he rubs hard circles on his sternum. "Hey, man. Come on, wake up. Can you tell me your name?"

A deep groan escapes his lips before he offers a shaky response. "Stephen. My name's Stephen." His speech is slurred. "What the fuck is going on?" His eyes dart around the room as if he doesn't remember where he is.

"Alright, Stephen. Calm down. We're only here to help. What drugs did you take?"

"No man." He's become agitated. "I wasn't doing no drugs. I just fell asleep, that's all."

As if he's heard that line before, the EMT working on Stephen blows out an exasperated breath. "Come on, Stephen. I can't help you if I don't know what you've taken. Make it easy and tell me now so I can get you to the hospital."

"It was just some weed. Maybe something else, I can't remember." His voice trails off with his admission.

"Alright, Stephen. We're going to lift you onto the gurney and get you to the hospital." The EMT turns to his partner who's busy working on Leslie. "This guy's ready to be transported. I'll be right back." He shouts towards the doorway where a third EMT is standing next to a gurney. "Hey, Bax. Come help me get him moved." As a team, the two men lift Stephen onto the gurney and quickly wheel him out of the room.

Leslie has her shirt pulled wide open. The attending paramedic rubs her sternum, just as the other did with Stephen. But unlike Stephen's quick response, Leslie isn't waking up. "Can you hear me?" He looks up to me. "What's your sister's name?"

"I-It's Leslie." My voice cracks. "Will she be alright?" I'm terrified I'm going to lose her.

He places his fingers on Leslie's carotid artery. "Her pulse is weak. We need to get her to the hospital as soon as possible."

A rush of emotions slam through my body. "Come on, Leslie, don't you dare give up." I watch closely as he opens a side pouch on his large medical bag, pulling out a small white box.

"Do you have any idea what drug she may have used tonight?"

"No, but I know she uses heroine sometimes and has been caught with oxycodone in the past. Does that help?"

"Yeah." He tears open the box and removes a T-shaped object, holding it between his thumb and two fingers like a syringe. "This nasal spray should help." The EMT tilts Leslie's head back, inserts the tip into her nostril and squeezes the plunger. When nothing happens, he grabs another spray and repeats the steps, this time up her left nostril.

Almost immediately, Leslie's eyes pop open as if she's been woken from a nightmare. A moment ago, she was unconscious and suddenly she's very much alert. I feel like I've been pulled into a scene from ER.

"Where am I? Where's my baby?" Leslie struggles against the paramedic while he continues working on her.

"Oh, my God, Leslie, Rory's right here. She's safe. I have her." I shout out my questions, hoping one of the EMT's will answer me. "What did you give her? What happened? Is she going to be okay?"

Leslie stops trying to push away the EMT's hands and falls silent.

The EMT continues to work as he speaks to me. "It's Narcan. A drug that blocks the effects of the opioids she took. Basically, it jumpstarts her brain and should keep her breathing while we transport her to the hospital. There's no guarantee she'll survive but at least it gives her a better chance."

Leslie's eyes are closed again. She looks fast asleep. The two paramedics hurriedly strap her limp body to a backboard and carry her toward the door. One of them speaks over his shoulder to let me know where they are taking her. "She'll be at Oceanside Hospital."

With all the chaos surrounding me, I fail to notice the two male police officers standing on the opposite side of the room. A squelch over one of their radios catches my attention. The shorter of the two officers speaks into the mic secured to the shoulder of his uniform.

"We're on scene. Two adults, one male, one female. Apparent overdose. The male is on his way to Highland. The female is being transported to Oceanside after Narcan was administered."

He pauses before continuing his relay of information. His earpiece keeps me from hearing the other side of the conversation. I pay special attention when he mentions Rory.

"10-4, Juvenile on scene. Female juvenile is approximately two or three years old. Dispatch Child Protective Services. She's responsive, no apparent injuries."

My nerves are shot to shit. If I wasn't leaning against the wall for support my knees would have buckled. Thank God I made it here in time for Rory and Leslie. Thoughts of what I could have walked in on has me on the edge of a panic attack.

I take a cleansing breath to calm myself and instantly regret it. I start gagging again on the smell that seems to be getting worse the longer I'm in the room. Now I know why. To my left is a box overflowing with old diapers. My god! They live like pigs.

Hoping to get outside and away from this god-awful stench, I speak up, attempting to draw the attention of one of the officers. "Excuse me officer...um...Sir?"

He turns toward me, shining his light in my direction. The room is dim but with the glow from his flashlight, I can see his brass name badge, Deputy L. Malloy. "I'm sorry, ma'am, but may I ask who you are and why you're here?"

"My name is Kellie Bryant. I'm Rory's aunt and sister to the woman who was just taken to the hospital."

"Thank you, Ms. Bryant. I'm Deputy Malloy. I'll need to ask you some more questions. What brought you here, ma'am?" His deep, official tone is somewhat intimidating.

"When I didn't hear from Leslie for two days, I came and busted the door to get in. Can I take Rory with me now? I want to get her settled, bathed and fed."

"No, I'm sorry but not yet. We need to take a few pictures for evidence, then she'll need to go to the hospital. Child Protective Services will have to be involved so it will take some time to get the emergency custody order straightened out." His response sounds cold and lacks emotion.

"CPS is useless. I've asked them for help getting Rory out of here for months and nothing." I stop myself from ranting to the one person who's finally helping me. "Sorry, I know you're only doing your job. I shouldn't take it out on you. I'm just anxious to get her out of here."

Even though Rory is underweight and small for her age, my arms are starting to ache from holding her securely against my chest for so long. Propping up her bottom causes my muscles to scream in protest. I notice the sleeve of my jacket is soaked with urine from the wet diaper. Ignoring the pain in my bicep, I rub circles with my right hand on her back and bounce her lightly, making a whispered shushing sound to keep her calm.

Rory turns her head away from my neck and begins sucking on her thumb. According to my mom, when Leslie was a little girl, she had the same habit. Mom says Rory will grow out of it, just like her momma did. I silently pray Leslie will survive and be around to see her daughter reach that simple milestone along with all the others as she grows up.

Please God, let Leslie be okay. I know she's not perfect but don't take her from us.

Deputy Malloy adjusts his hat and exhales. He appears

frustrated. "I know you want to get her out of here, but you need to wait for the ambulance. We still have evidence to gather before you leave."

"Okay, I'm sorry. I just hate this whole damn thing." My voice is shaky and my body trembles as I crash from the earlier adrenaline rush.

"It's fine. You have nothing to be sorry for. You'll have to excuse me for being so gruff. It drives me crazy when there are kids involved in a mess like this. I shouldn't have spoken to you so rudely. I apologize." He hands me a cotton handkerchief and I wipe my eyes then Rory's face.

"I don't think you were rude, Deputy. I can only imagine the things you see. I'm glad you're here for us today. Thank you." I offer him the handkerchief back.

"You can keep it, I have plenty."

Two more officers arrive, moving throughout the apartment, gathering evidence in little plastic bags and taking more pictures. Flashlights blind me as officers snap pictures from all angles. Luckily, Rory is entertained by them and is babbling happily.

"Bright light." Rory sounds like an alien when she speaks but I'm able to pick up what she is saying easily.

"Deputy Malloy? Would it be alright to go into the bedroom and get her cleaned up? I mean if that's okay?"

"Sure, but I need to come with you."

While the other officers continue to search the apartment, Deputy Malloy never leaves our side. I assume he's staying close because he has no idea who I really am. It's his job to protect Rory and that means not letting us out of his sight. Instead of being annoyed, I'm grateful he's here to keep her safe.

We walk to the bedroom where I found Rory screaming for Leslie earlier. Deputy Malloy switches on the overhead light illuminating the space. This room isn't quite as messy as the rest of the apartment but still filthy. I turn back to the officer, not sure what to say about the appearance of the room.

He's removed his Deputy Sheriff ball cap, tucked it under his arm and appears to be scanning the area. Without his hat on, I can see more of Deputy Malloy's features. His eye color surprises me, more of a grey than blue. His typical law enforcement style haircut is too closely shaved for me to tell what color it really is. A strong, masculine jawline is dusted with a touch of stubble. He looks every inch the professional, clean cut law enforcement officer in appearance.

"I guess I shouldn't be surprised that this room looks like the rest of the place. Where do you want to change her?" The deputy's tone is flat, almost emotionless.

Rory speaks more words neither of us can figure out. I guess I'll need to learn how to decipher toddler talk while Leslie goes to rehab.

"If you say so kiddo." He responds to Rory's gibberish. His kindness makes me smile. She squirms and twists in my arms. I turn her to face Deputy Malloy, anchoring her back to my chest with one arm under her bottom and the other around her belly. She reaches out as if she wants the officer to hold her.

Of course, I don't expect him to take her but what he does next surprises me. The kind deputy continues his mainly one-way conversation with Rory. He speaks to her in a soothing, calm tone. "Who's a brave little princess?" She looks up at him with more jumbled words, holding on to the finger he let her grab onto. I watch the two of them, grateful for the moment of calm it's brought over me as well.

"Alright, sweet princess. You need to let go of my finger so your aunt can get you dressed. Can you do that for me?"

His teasing grants him the sweetest smile.

"Yeth." Hearing her respond and able to understand warms my heart.

His shoulders shake, and his duty belt keys jingle when he laughs.

"Can I take her over to the bed, change her diaper and put her in clean clothes?" She's soaked and filthy. I have no idea when she was last fed either. I'm embarrassed at how badly my sister treated Rory. The bed is covered in various stains and so many cigarette burns, I'm surprised the place never burned down.

"Sure, hang on and let me grab a clean blanket from my trunk." He calls out for another officer to come to the room while he goes to his patrol car.

Deputy Malloy returns quickly with a stuffed bear tucked under his arm and a plastic wrapped blanket in hand. He tears open the wrapper and spreads the thin fabric over the old comforter. When he holds the teddy bear out for Rory to see, she grabs on to it, and bites down on his stitched nose.

"Hang on, Rory. Let's give that back so I can get you changed." I hand the bear back to the officer who uses it to keep Rory's attention, shaking it above where she lays. She seems mesmerized by the bear being held just out of reach. I pull the soiled onesie carefully over Rory's head before throwing it to the side near the trash can. Tears of frustration fall down my cheeks and drip on Rory's belly. I wipe them away with the back of my hand. *Why did I wait so long to come over here?*

I keep my focus on Rory, stroking her cheek lightly with my fingertips, before speaking. "You must think I'm a terrible person to leave my niece here in this mess for so long."

"I don't think that at all. The system doesn't make it easy to remove children from neglectful parents. And who suffers? The ones who can't speak for themselves yet may carry the trauma and emotional scars for life. Even my hands are tied when it comes to how much I can do."

"Yes, but I should have tried harder to get her out of

here." My shame keeps me from looking up while I confess my perceived failure.

"Ms. Bryant, you followed the chain of command and trusted they would be there to protect your niece. You did nothing wrong. I have no doubt you'll take care of Rory, the way her mother should have done."

"Thank you. I needed to hear that. And you're right. From this moment on, my life will be dedicated to creating a new world for Rory. Hopefully, she's too young to remember any of the bad things she has experienced so far."

"With your help, I'm sure she'll be okay."

"I love my niece and sister and plan to help Leslie find a way out of her addiction and remain a part of her daughter's life." A wave of anxiety washes over me as I remember what Leslie looked like as they brought her to the ambulance. "Do you think Leslie will be okay? Have you heard anything?"

"No, I'm sorry. I haven't heard anything over the radio. They are both very lucky to have you. I can see what an amazing woman you are. Instead of being angry and bitter, you're already thinking about how to make a life better for you all."

"Oh, trust me, I'm angry and when Leslie gets home, she's going to hear about it, but what good will it do to rage about it now?"

"Addy K." Rory interrupts the moment by saying her version of Auntie Kellie. She's reaching out with grabby hands, still wanting the bear dangling from above.

"Alright girlie, let's finish getting you changed." Placing my hand on Rory's tummy so she doesn't get up, I nod with a head tilt towards the pink dresser against the wall. "Would you mind handing me a diaper and wipes from the top drawer?"

I watch him use his bright flashlight to dig around in the drawer then hand me a disposable diaper and almost empty pack of wipes. It's a miracle they haven't dried out.

KAYLEE ROSE

He continues his search through each drawer, cursing under his breath. "Damn it. I can't believe this shit. There are so many new clothes in here and the tags are still on most of them. I'm sorry, I shouldn't swear but this makes no sense."

I look past him to see the clothes he's referring to. "Trust me, I understand your frustration. I bought most of those outfits last month. She was probably going to sell them or try to return them for drug money." I blow out a breath and my shoulders slump with the feeling of failure. "Rory has been through so much. I tried to get custody, but Child Protective Services and the courts shut me down each time."

"I'd like to say I'm surprised, but that would be a lie."

A quick wash with the wet wipes will have to do until I get her home. I tape up the sides of the disposable diaper and toss the old one in the overflowing garbage can. Before I can reach for clean clothes, the officer beats me to it by shining his flashlight on a dress with an image of *Sleeping Beauty* on the front surrounded by her three fairies flying around protecting her from the evil villain, *Maleficent*.

"How about this one?" Deputy Malloy's choice of dress and smirk gives away a bit more of his personality.

"Sure, that will work. I think there are some shoes in there too. Can you grab them please?"

He paws through the drawers when he finally finds what he's been searching for. "Our little princess here needs some glass slippers too." He holds up the oversized pair of clear plastic dress up shoes I bought Rory for her birthday last year. I knew they'd be too big as they are meant for a child five and up, but I couldn't resist buying them for her.

"No glass slippers for Rory today. Those are for dress up time. Can you grab those small white ones on the top shelf?"

"Found them." He holds them up for me to see.

When I take the shoes from him, they look tiny in his large hands. "Thanks. Oh, and you do know it's *Cinderella* that wears the glass slippers, not *Sleeping Beauty*, right?"

18

"Yeah, I know, but after everything this little one's gone through, she's extra special and gets to be whoever she wants to be." Deputy Malloy's smile is so big, I notice the dimples pop in his cheeks. He really is a handsome man. For a moment, the gravity of the situation is lessened somewhat, and it seems we both let our guard down.

The playful expression Deputy Malloy had didn't last long. His mood shifts instantly when the red and blue flashing lights appear through the doorway. The professional side to him snapping back into place.

"It's time to get Rory to the hospital. You can go in the ambulance with her." He answers my question before I have time to ask.

He hands Rory the stuffed bear and walks behind us while I carry Rory down the rickety stairs and into the back of the waiting ambulance.

"Deputy Malloy, I can never thank you enough for making this horrible experience a little easier." I look down to Rory who's snuggling the bear and turn my attention back to the officer.

"You're very welcome, Ms. Bryant. Take care of little Rory. I hope your sister recovers."

As the door to the ambulance closes, I tug the blanket and tuck it under Rory's chin. My exhausted niece is now fast asleep, still clutching the bear. Most importantly, she's safe now.

Emotionally exhausted, the events of the last few hours hit me full on as tears slide down my cheeks. I silently thank god for watching over Rory and pray Leslie will be okay too. No matter what tomorrow brings, life will never be the same for any of us. I only hope I'm strong enough to overcome the mountain of obstacles that undoubtedly lie ahead.

Upon arriving at the hospital, Rory and I were taken to a private room. Both doctors and nurses checked her over for physical injury, took blood and finally cleared her.

Child Protective Services were waiting for us. The officer was able to obtain an emergency order, allowing me to take her home.

"How is Leslie?" I asked.

"Somebody will be along to talk to you soon." I felt it was a brush off, but exhausted, I climbed onto the gurney with Rory, snuggling close.

A knock on the partially open-door startles me from my sleep. A woman in a white lab coat covering pink hospital scrubs comes into the room.

"Oh, shoot, I didn't mean to fall asleep. I'm sorry. Do you need to check Rory again?" I shift a sleeping Rory to the middle of the bed and scoot myself into a sitting position.

"Hi, Kellie, I'm Dr. Greene." She has kind eyes. "You're fine." Flipping through the folder she's holding she mumbles to herself. My heart is in my mouth. "It looks like you've both been through a lot tonight." She casts a glance at my sleeping niece. "She's a cutie." Closing the file, she steps closer. "I spoke with Rory's doctor. He's signing her discharge papers now. Is someone coming to take you home?"

"Yes, I called my parents, they're on their way. Do you know what's going on with my sister, Leslie Taylor?"

"That's actually why I'm here. If you want, I can wait until your parent's arrive to update you on your sister." Dr. Greene's eyes soften as her voice trails off.

If this is bad news, it will be better if I tell my parents. "Please don't wait. I need to know what's going on."

"Alright." She's obviously uncomfortable. "I attended to Leslie when she was brought into the ER. She was unconscious and didn't respond to any of the medications or stimulus we provided." She pauses before delivering the news I feared most. "I'm so sorry, Ms. Taylor, but Leslie didn't make it." Hearing the doctor's words knocks the air from my lungs.

Dr. Green reaches out to touch my hand. "I wish I had

better news. Would you like me to have someone come sit with you until your parents arrive?"

"No, um, I'll be fine. Oh, God. She's really gone." I must be in shock because I can't cry. Not because I don't care, but because I know breaking down right now won't help and I need to figure out how I'm going to tell my parents.

Dr Greene is talking but I don't hear what she is saying. Does anything else she has to say really matter? Leslie's dead and part of my heart died with her.

"Your parents are here," she advises. "Would you like me to stay?"

"No. Thank you. I think it's best if they hear it from me."

"Okay, I'll have the nurse bring them in. If you need anything, please ask the nurse to find me."

All I can manage is a simple nod as the tears I've been fighting begin to fall down my cheeks.

"Addy K?" Rory calls my name and reaches out to be held.

I gladly lift my still sleepy niece into my arms, cradling her against my chest and whisper, "What are we going to do without your momma?"

"Momma." Rory repeats my last word, bringing on a new wave of heartbreak and tears. She turns into my chest and pops her thumb into her mouth.

It's time to pull myself together. I use the handkerchief Deputy Malloy gave me to wipe my eyes and get ready to deliver the news of Leslie's death to my parents.

Just as Rory's eyes begin to close, my parents are escorted into the room.

Both Mom and Dad are pale faced. Their terror is palpable. They have seconds until I'm forced to break their hearts and blow their world wide open.

"Kellie, what's wrong?" Mom asks. "You said Rory is fine, but where's Leslie?" She speaks so fast I can barely keep up.

"You said they were both here." Her voice shakes while she frantically looks outside the doorway.

"Mom, please sit down. Dad you too." They follow my directions, slowly lowering themselves into the couch set up for visitors. They clutch each others hands. They know what is coming even though neither want to admit it.

This doesn't feel real. I do my best to stay strong for my family, hugging my niece tight against my chest like a security blanket. "I don't know how to do this. Nothing I say will make it easier for you." I pause to gather my thoughts before steeling my resolve to just say it. "Leslie is dead. She overdosed and they couldn't save her this time." Mom's mouth drops open, but I can't read my Dad at all. "I tried to get her here as soon as possible. It's my fault. I should have been there sooner. If I hadn't waited two days, I could have saved her. I'm so sorry." I turn my head in shame, not able to look at the hurt I know must be in their eyes.

"No!" My Dad finally speaks up. "This can't be true. Where is she? I want to see her. Where's my daughter..." Dad's voice is laced with pain as he shouts his demands to see Leslie. My usually stoic father pulls my mom onto his arms, holding her tight just as I'm holding Rory. Each of us comforting yet drawing strength from the person in our arms.

Dad falls silent, tears running down his cheeks, shushing and rocking mom while her sobs combine with my own. We've lost Leslie and right now, in this moment, I don't know how we'll move on without her in our lives.

3

LANCE

Driving home after working a twelve-hour shift for the Springhill County Sheriff's Department, I think of what I want to do tonight. Change out of this uniform, grab a cold beer, heat up some of last night's pizza and sit under the stars in my hot tub. Hell, I'm so exhausted, I may not even heat the pizza. Thankfully it's a short drive from the station to my house.

I park my truck in the driveway, turn off the ignition and tilt my head back on the headrest while I attempt the transition from work to home mode. On a deep breath, I close my eyes, thankful for another day I made it home safe.

As much as I want to stay home, my plans for a quiet night will have to wait. The team I work with have different plans. A special meeting has been called by my work brothers and sisters. They are my 'Family of Blue'. My fellow first responders who I work with and depend upon daily. Tonight, we'll gather at our usual place, Heath's Bar and Grill.

Hanging out, away from work, allows us to relax and leave the job behind, if only for a few hours. It provides us with a sense of normality we don't often have.

There are things learned and seen through my training,

and real-life events that have changed my view of what normal is. I look through different eyes now and see things others may not notice.

For instance, in the past, I could wander aimlessly through a crowded county fair, oblivious to my surroundings. Now, I notice the heated discussion off to the side of the soda booth. I see the suspicious person with eyes darting around the vendor tables as if ready to steal the trinkets on display. My training never switches off, and that's a good thing. I need to be on constant alert to be good at what I do. Being vigilant keeps the public, myself, and my family safe.

But when I'm not in uniform, it would be nice to turn it off occasionally. Unfortunately, it doesn't always work that way. My dad tried telling me about the changes to expect in my life. Every officer begins their career wide-eyed and eager to face the world. The change is slow and deceptive and usually only noticed by friends and family. I didn't understand what he meant until I experienced it for myself. Now it's just part of who I am.

Tonight, instead of relaxing in my hot tub, I'll be with my work family giving and receiving the support we all need.

When I walk into the house, I head straight to my bedroom, peeling off my uniform and trauma vest. The ripping sound of the *Velcro* branded fastener signals my brain to slow down. Next, I remove my duty belt with gear attached, instantly feeling fifty pounds lighter. I move everything to my closet, locking up my gun and extra magazines in the large safe hidden behind the racks of clothes. Only recently did I realize this routine is almost the same as my father's. Only where he came home to my mom and me, my house is empty.

I undress, hang my uniform, and toss the remainder of my clothes into the hamper. One of the benefits of living alone;

after I fully strip down, I don't have to put on clothes to walk around my own house.

Buck ass naked, I walk down the hall to the kitchen to have the pizza that's been calling my name. I didn't eat lunch, but that's not unusual. We don't have as much down time as you may think.

Without bothering to turn on the light, I pull on the refrigerator door to open it. There isn't much in here except a cardboard pizza box, expired milk, some juice, and a few random condiments. I stack two slices of cold pizza on top of one another and wolf it down in just a few bites, chasing it with the orange juice straight from the carton. That should hold me over until I get to Heath's.

I stretch my arms above my head while walking back to the master bathroom. A glance in the mirror above the vanity causes me to pause and inspect my five o'clock shadow. It's not too bad. The scruff can wait until I shave tomorrow morning before work.

Turning the shower handle up, I step under the cold spray before the water warms. Cooling down after wearing my gear all day feels good and hopefully will help wake me up, providing me the energy to make it through tonight's meeting. When the water heats up, I turn around, the massaging action pounding the muscles in my back.

As much as I hate to admit it, I'm glad to be getting out of the house tonight. Tomorrow will be my first day off in ten days. Being short staffed has everyone working extra hours. It's been months since I went on a date. Hiding away in the house isn't going to rectify that situation. Unfortunately, finding a woman I want to spend time with isn't as easy as it sounds.

My work schedule isn't the regular Monday through Friday nine to five. A holiday for everyone else is just another workday for me.

My last girlfriend thought she could handle dating a LEO,

Law Enforcement Officer. It only took a few months of unexpected changes, cancelled dates and her constantly worrying about my safety to drive a wedge between us.

Her tolerance for my job came to an end the very day I was to meet her parents at their anniversary party. An emergency at work interrupted our plans requiring me to report to the station immediately. Dialing Patricia's number, I prepared myself for another angry rant about how my job always comes first.

"Lance!" There was no mistaking her anger in the high-pitched tone of her voice. "You've got to be fucking kidding me."

"I'm sorry, hon, but–" She wasn't in the mood to listen to anything I had to say.

"Why can't someone else take your place?" Patricia's screech was laced with anger, causing me to hold the phone away from my ear.

"Come on, babe, you know how this works. I don't have the luxury of choosing when an emergency fucks up my plans. Two deputies were injured in a chase tonight. We're short staffed. I'm sorry, but there's no way I'm going to be able to make it to the party tonight."

"Don't you dare *babe* me. You can tell them to call someone else in. What about your partner Paul? You're always telling me how you have each other's back, ask him to do it."

Patricia always falls back on Paul, blaming him for the extra hours I work. "He's not available. I've told you why, so you need to back off." I pace around my bedroom, running my fingers through my hair in frustration. "I'm not sure what you want from me."

"Nothing Lance. I want nothing. Not tonight or any other night for that matter. We're done. I won't come second to any job."

She hung up before I could respond. Not having time to

call her back and argue, I decide to give her time to calm down. I planned to call her in the morning but before my shift ended my phone blew up with multiple texts as she unleashed her wrath upon me.

I didn't respond, mainly because I understood her frustration. It was obvious she wasn't the woman I was meant to be with for the rest of my life. Her outrageous behavior in the months following our breakup made it abundantly clear breaking up was for the best.

Finding a time and place to meet someone new is the obstacle I face now. Usually the local bars are full of badge bunnies. Those women just looking for a hook-up with a cop. There was a time when I would take the bunnies up on their offers, but it got old quick.

The water starts to cool, a reminder I need to get moving so I'm not late.

After quickly soaping up and rinsing off, I grab the towel from the rack on the wall and wrap it around my waist. I give my teeth a quick brush, swipe on deodorant and add a splash of cologne. With a finger comb to my short hair, I look in the mirror again. That's good enough. Now for some old jeans, a black t-shirt, socks, and boots.

Lastly, I grab my watch, wallet, and keys off the dining table and head out to spend an evening blowing off steam.

The bar is only a few miles from my house. I don't plan on drinking tonight but if I change my mind and decide to have a few beers, it's close enough to walk home or I can use one of the designated drivers we set up ahead of time.

When I pull into the gravel lot, I recognize a few of the trucks and cars as those of my team. I'm glad to see I'm not the first one here.

Parked outside the bar, I see a black stretch limousine.

Either there's a VIP in here tonight, which is highly unlikely, or it's exactly what I fear it may be.

"Fuck!" A closer look at the limo gives me a view of the blow-up penis sticking out of the sunroof. It's a bachelorette party. Great!

Some of the men and women in my department love it when bachelorette's have their last hurrah at Heath's. I don't. Drunk and overly flirtatious ladies aren't my style at all. Once they find out we're cops, the lewd comments and flirting begins.

Will you use your handcuffs on me? Want to frisk me? I'd love a full body cavity search.

Or the one I hate the most. How big is your weapon? Which is usually followed by a crotch grab.

Hopefully tonight will be different and I'll be able to relax and enjoy the evening with my buddies without any awkward moments.

4

KELLIE

Every day I thank god for following my instincts and now Rory is safe, happy, and content living with me as her guardian.

It seems a lifetime ago, but it's only been a little over six months and a lot has changed in that time. The building my sister Leslie and Rory lived in was condemned shortly after the incident and is now an empty lot.

Today is full of errands, topped off with Rory's appointment with her doctor for a routine physical and influenza vaccination. I get more nervous about these appointments than Rory does.

Nurse Gloria knocks on the door carrying a tray with the syringe and small vial of medication. "Alright, Rory. Are you ready? I'm going to give you some medicine, so you don't get sick and when I'm done, you can pick a prize from the treasure chest."

Gloria has worked alongside Rory's pediatrician, Dr. Michaelson for years. Together they make a great team. Their friendly smiles and compassionate hearts helped get me through those first few appointments when I was certain every single thing I did was wrong. Gloria urged me to follow my instincts, gave me a list of websites to research and walked me through a few of the more difficult parts of raising and caring for a toddler. "You'll do just fine. That little girl loves you and feels safe, everything else will come in time, you just wait and see." Those few words of encouragement set my mind at ease.

Dr. Michaelson reassured me too. "Don't worry, Kellie. Every new parent has these same concerns. I have no doubt you will be an amazing parent and remember Gloria and I are here to help."

Patting the vacant examination table, Gloria reminds Rory what to do. "Climb up here and face Aunt Kellie."

Rory bounces up on the table, spins on her bottom so her left shoulder is in position for the shot and says, "Ready."

Nurse Gloria washes her hands, pulls on a pair of purple latex gloves and turns to the exam table with the tray.

Gloria has a unique way of distracting Rory while giving her the immunizations. She has Rory pretend to be a big gust of wind, blowing the paper origami swans which hang above the exam table. "Okay, Rory. Here we go. Deep breath in, hold it, and blow."

My little trooper squeezes her eyes shut, puffs her cheeks out with air and blows it out just as the needle pierces her skin. Nurse Gloria is the master at giving injections because although Rory flinches, she didn't shed a single tear. I on the other hand had to turn away as dust has drifted into my eyes causing them to water. Well, that's my story and I'm sticking to it.

After Gloria applies a *Sesame Street Band-Aid* to Rory's shoulder, she hands me a tissue. "Here you go, Aunt Kellie. It sure does get dusty in here." There's no fooling her. She chuckles and turns to Rory. "You did great. Now get dressed and Aunt Kellie will take you to the toy chest."

A pirate's eye patch was her treasure today. She was

begging me to put it on her before we could make our way out of the doctor's office.

Instead of driving straight home after her appointment, we opted to pick up some snacks and have a picnic in the park. When Rory finished eating her grape jelly *Crustables* sandwich and carrot sticks, she played with the other kids at the playground shouting Argh Matey, pretending to sword fight the imaginary crocodile from *Peter Pan* for almost an hour.

My secret plan to wear her out before we get home appears to be working. I watch Rory as she walks wearily toward me, dragging her feet. She crawls up into my lap and says, "Addy K, I sleepy," followed by a huge yawn. I kiss her forehead and whisper, "You must be exhausted after your battle with the evil crocodile. Are you ready to go home sleepyhead?"

When I glance down, my pirate princess has already fallen fast asleep. Rather than take her to the car right away, I sit and enjoy the fresh air. After all the errands and appointments of the day, it feels good to slow down and reflect.

Looking down at the angelic face of this little girl who has become my whole world opens the special place in my heart where I keep Leslie and her memory alive.

Rory reminds me so much of her momma. They share many traits. If I close my eyes I can still see the faces Leslie would pull, those same facial expressions I see from Rory now. A pouty lip when they didn't get their own way and eyes squeezed tight shut with bright smiles when happy. I choose to think about the good memories I had with my sister, rather than the dark times leading up to her death. Those are the ones I want to share with Rory.

I can only imagine how torn my parents must feel, losing their eldest daughter so suddenly. If I were to lose Rory, my life would crumble. I suppose having Rory as a link to Leslie has helped ease some of the grief for all of us.

It's time to get home so I can get dinner started. Tonight is mac and cheese, again. Rory isn't a fan of vegetables, so I sneak them in where possible. With a shift of Rory's limp exhausted body to my left shoulder, I awkwardly sling my tote over my other shoulder and walk to my car.

While Rory naps, I tiptoe down the hall to check on her. Her bedroom door is slightly ajar allowing me to peer inside without being noticed. She has kicked off her blankets and is stretched across the bed like a starfish.

My cellphone vibrates in my pocket.

"Ugh." It's my best friend Gina, no doubt reminding me once again about her bachelorette party. As if I can forget. It is etched deep into my mind, just as our time together at college is. As two terrified students, living away from home for the first time, we leaned heavily on each other for support.

It was junior year, just after our final exams. We celebrated by scarfing down a huge tub of chocolate ice cream, drinking too much tequila and discussing the future. We were very drunk and talked a lot of crazy shit, including the promise to act as maid of honor for each other when the time came.

When Dirk proposed, Gina called, squealing with excitement, and reminded me of that night, asking if I was ready to stand by her side.

My maid of honor duties are simple. For the most part I fluff Gina's dress before she walks down the aisle, stand at the altar, and hold her flowers during the exchange of rings. The only duty, or chore I've been dreading is tonight's party.

With bare feet, I pad through our tiny kitchen to grab my coffee cup from the microwave and continue into the living room. In the corner of the room is a big overstuffed chair facing out the large bay window. It's my favorite spot to read, relax, and for today, figure out how I'm going to worm my way out of tonight's festivities. I sink into the fluffy cushions, tucking my feet under me. After a few sips of the sweet, creamy hazelnut coffee, I figure it's time to face the music and see what Gina needs.

Using my thumb to unlock the screen I cringe when I see the number of missed calls and texts. I scroll through without really reading before checking my voicemail. While listening to the last message from Gina, she strikes a raw nerve.

"Come on, Kellie. You *need* this night out. You're too young to stay home every night watching cartoons on *Netflix*. It's my bachelorette party, my last night as a single woman. It won't be the same without you."

I understand why she wants me to get out more, but I really don't understand the whole *last night as a single woman* thing. When you decide to dedicate your life to another person, why do you want to have one last night pretending to be single? It's not the memory I want before my wedding day.

In my fantasy, my fiancé sneaks into my room the night before our vows, breaking all tradition, because he can't stand the thought of being away from me for even that one night. I have the whole ceremony planned too. My wedding will be at sunset with just a few friends and Rory standing by my side. My prince charming will be there, staring into my eyes, declaring his love for me as well as his dedication to be everything Rory needs. I'm a package deal and won't accept anything less than a man who loves us both.

Thinking about my fantasy wedding always brings me back to the same person.

Deputy Malloy of the Springhill Sheriff's Department is the man I see in my dreams. It's crazy, I know, but the officer who helped me the night I rescued Rory is the one I envision standing beside me. His caring personality and the tender way he treated Rory is what makes my heart flip-flop. I confess, the uniform is hot too, and oh man, did he wear it well.

It is a silly crush because he was only doing his job.

Shaking my head at my own stupidity, I know I need to get over him or I'm going to be single for the rest of my life. Still, I'm not sure anyone can live up to the man I've created in my imagination.

A hummingbird zips past the window pulling me out of my prince charming daydream. Tonight isn't about *my* happy ever after, and I need to decide if I'm going to celebrate with the girls or stay home and watch TV just as Gina predicts.

Before I can finish reading all her messages, my phone rings. I need to woman up and tell her I'm not coming tonight.

I answer her call, happy my decision is made.

"Hey Gina! I was just going through your texts and was about to call you."

"Well, now you don't have to. You're all set for the party, right?" Her confidence, and belief she's getting her own way irritates me further.

"Gina, I know you want me to come tonight, but I don't have a babysitter."

"You've known about this for ages."

"I know, but–"

"No buts, Kell–"

"Go and have fun without me and I'll meet you at your mom's in the morning." I want to add hangover free, but refrain. Just because I don't want to go doesn't mean I should ruin her fun.

"I knew you'd use the *I don't have a sitter excuse,* so I took matters into my own hands." She sounded far too pleased with herself. "I just left your mom's house and she said to get Rory ready because she'll be at your place in ten minutes to pick her up. Oh, she also added something else."

"What?" I was beyond annoyed at her interference.

"That you need to find a nice guy and get laid."

"Oh. My. God! She did not say that!" My mom can get

crazy at times, but I know she would never say anything like that, especially to Gina.

She's laughing so hard she sounds out of breath. "Okay, okay, maybe those weren't her exact words, but she strongly suggests I help you find a nice gentleman, but I say screw the gentleman part and go find some hot guy who can fuck you hard all night long."

I cringe having to listen to the filth that comes out of her foul mouth. Having a toddler around I try to keep cuss words to a minimum, so I bite my tongue instead of saying what I really want to say.

Gina continues barking her orders. "No more excuses. It's a done deal. Now find your cutest black dress, slip into some sexy heels, and let's get ready to make every man drool. My cousins bought a bunch of bachelorette crap."

"Oh, God," I groan.

"I've got penis suckers and headbands with bouncing cocks. I intend to say goodbye to being single in style."

Style. Right. A room full of women in skimpy, black dresses, all wearing cock headbands. Now that's classy. I wouldn't put it past them to have the tacky *bride to be* sash too. This will be a night to forget, more than remember.

It's obvious my excuses are falling flat and I'm not getting out of tonight's escapades. "Alright! I'll go! Rory's still taking a nap. I need to get her up and ready for my mom, then meet you at your apartment. What time's the limo going to be there?"

I pull my cell away from my ear when Gina lets out a loud, happy squeal. She loves to get her own way.

"It's scheduled to arrive at 7pm but get here early and don't try pulling that bullshit excuse you don't have anything sexy to wear. Get that special dress out of the back of the closet and wear the strappy heels I gave you for Christmas."

"Okay, bossy, I got it. Now let me check on Rory and get us both ready." I end the call and place my phone on the end table beside me. Little does Gina know, by getting her own way, she's going to owe me multiple hours of babysitting time.

My mom will be here soon, not giving me much wiggle room to wake Rory and gather her things. She doesn't take long to get moving which helps when we're in a hurry, just like now.

Unlike some children who wake up yelling and crying to get out of bed, Rory wakes up full of smiles with bright, happy eyes. Each time I see her smile, it's a special gift I don't ever want to take for granted, especially after the less than perfect start to her life.

When I open the door fully, I can see her staring silently at the stars glowing on the ceiling. After reading several books about the universe and hours of watching a silly movie about space dogs, she's become obsessed with constellations and planets. When I ask if she wants to be an astronaut like the doggies on TV, she pretends to fly around the room with her arms stretched out like wings.

Last month we read a book about a veterinarian and how he cares for sick animals. The basket of stuffed tigers, monkeys, horses, and other toys, all wrapped in bandages still sits in the corner of her room just in case she changes her mind again. Even her favorite bear still has a few band-aides stuck to his fur.

I open the door fully and tip toe up to her bed. After a few silent moments, she notices me and I whisper, "Hello, Sleeping Beauty. Did you have a good nap?"

She's all smiles and wiggles when I reach down and lift my sweet girl from her pink castle shaped bed. I may have gone a little overboard with the princess décor, but I'm living my childhood fantasies through Rory. I would have loved to sleep in this bed as a little girl.

"I wake up." She tells me this every time, and I wonder if she's asking a question or making a statement.

She has a limited vocabulary, often repeating the phrases she's become familiar with. When I first became aware she wasn't saying full sentences like the other kids at pre-school, I took her to see a speech therapist. The doctor explained how the trauma she endured, and the things she saw are partially responsible for her delayed speech.

The pediatrician and speech therapist both say she will catch up in time, but I need to be patient.

Before coming to live with me, it seems she didn't do much talking at all, so anything is a bonus.

We read a lot and work on her repeating my words all day long in the hope it speeds up the learning process. She understands what I tell her, and she follows directions as well as any three-year-old can, she just doesn't have much to say right now.

"Yes, you did wake up." I pull her in for a hug and spin around slowly before walking to her changing table. I sit her on the cushion and continue my running dialogue; the doctors said this will encourage her to talk more.

"Guess what baby girl? Gram Gram is coming to pick you up. You get to stay with her and Grumpa tonight."

"Gram Gram, Grumpa." The excitement in her voice makes me feel better about going out with the girls. She loves spending time with her grandparents, just as they welcome any time with her.

She made up the nicknames for everyone in her life, and they're too cute to correct. My father pretends he doesn't like Grumpa, but when he complains, Rory laughs and dances around repeating Grumpa until he gives in with a smile. I think he objects just to see Rory's antics.

"We need to finish getting dressed. Gram Gram will be here any minute." I pull the nightgown over her head and grab a fresh *Pull Up* from the shelf.

"I pee." She pulls on her wet diaper letting me know she hates how it feels. I doubt Leslie ever tried potty training

Rory. My guess is it was easier to keep accepting the free diapers rather than take time away from getting high to teach her. Oh, and selling the diapers for drug money was just an added incentive. Each morning we talk about wearing big girl panties and using the potty instead of diapers and *Pull-Ups.*

"Yes, you did. Maybe it's time to start using the super cool potty Gram Gram gave you. The one that plays songs when you pee in it." I've tried a few times but when she became too frustrated, we took a break. I'm ready to start again when she is.

Rory's face is scrunched up like she's thinking really hard. Or maybe she's got to poop? I really hope it's the latter. "Addy K, no potty."

She may not say much, but what she does say gets her point across. I guess it's not time for the potty yet. I tickle her tummy, just so I can hear her giggles.

She's so smart, I just wish she would say more. I can see her little brain working overtime, but for now her world is full of simple phrases, pointing and an occasional grunt.

With her *Pull-Up* and undershirt in place we move on to the next important decision. Which princess should she be today? I hold up two dresses for her to choose from. "Which will it be? Are you *Ariel* or *Cinderella* today?"

Mimicking one of my bad habits, she taps her index finger against her chin, while trying to decide, then tells me her choice. *"Aurora."*

Of course, she doesn't go with either of my dress options, but the fact she didn't just repeat my words is a step in the right direction. *"Sleeping Beauty,* it is."

"Sing prince will come? Pweez?"

How can I resist that face? "Okay but let me put these other dresses away first."

"Sing, Addy K, sing!" She claps and bounces on her bottom while begging for her favorite *Disney* princess song.

"Fine, but you have to sing with me."

"Someday my…" was as far as I got before Rory shouts out the word prince, causing us both to dissolve into a fit of giggles.

I start the song again, both of us singing completely off-key. My heart melts when I hear her sing the word prince again. It is all she can manage before she hums the rest of the lyrics. Eventually she will be able to sing the whole song with me.

"We need to hurry up, I think I hear Gram Grams car."

Planting a kiss on Rory's chubby cheek, I buckle her safely into her car seat, and send her off for a wonderful night with my parents. Now it's time to get myself ready.

Before I talk myself out of going, I gather the things I need for tonight. There are a hundred reasons I should change into my PJ's, blow off the bachelorette party and another hundred why this party is exactly what I need.

If I keep arguing with myself, I know which side will win—the responsible, always need to stay in control woman I became when I accepted Rory as my number one priority. This is the first time I'm even considering going out for a girl's night since Rory moved in with me.

My life was turned upside down the day I found her crying in her crib. Although I was angry and frustrated with Leslie, I loved my big sister and always will. Growing up I wanted to be just like her, copying everything she did right down to how she dressed.

"You're just like a mini-me," she would often say, allowing me to tag along wherever she went. When the older girls would complain about my presence, Leslie would put them in their place, always protecting me. I only wish I could have protected her the same way.

As usually happens, we hit our teens and went our separate ways, finding new friends and different interests. I was so into my own life I didn't see what Leslie was going through, how much she'd changed, until it was too late.

My offers to help were ignored as the addiction held her in a tight grip, refusing to let go. I hated her for not trying harder.

Initially, I blamed everyone for Leslie's death. Myself, the doctors, the courts that did nothing to help, and especially my parents. I hated them for not listening when I told them Leslie was sneaking out of the house and cutting classes to get high. If they had just listened to me then, maybe my sister would still be alive.

Leslie had everyone fooled as a teenager and became more adept at deception as the years went by.

After Rory was born, she would show up for Sunday lunch acting and pretending life was perfect. Rory would be dressed in one of the new outfits I'd purchased for her while Leslie would appear sober and responsible although I could see she had taken something to keep my parents from seeing what was really going on.

At some point when Leslie thought I was out of earshot, she would mention needing money for rent, utilities, formula or diapers and my parents would hand over the cash without any questions.

It was all bullshit. She lived in subsidized housing which covered her utilities. She received free diapers and formula from the child welfare clinic. Leslie used that money for drugs and only came back to Mom and Dad's house when she ran out of drugs or cash.

Each time I tried to tell my parents Leslie was lying, they would turn on me, making me the bad guy.

"When are you going to see she's lying just to get money? You know she will only use it to buy drugs." I feel like a broken record. We have this argument every Sunday after dinner.

Mom would defend Leslie time and again. "Kellie, you don't know how hard it is to raise a child."

Yeah, well neither does Leslie.

"Maybe if you stop giving her cash, she won't be able to get high and we can get her the help she needs."

"Stop saying that about your sister. She's just going through a hard time trying to get by on her own. We are fortunate to be able to help her with some of the things Rory needs and it's not for you to judge me for doing it."

Throwing up my hands in defeat, I turn to my dad hoping he will finally hear me. "Can you please talk to your wife? Leslie is addicted to narcotics. I'm guessing she's tried a bit of everything. I've also smelled alcohol on her when I've stopped by in the early morning hours to check on Rory. Leslie is sick and needs our help. Until you stop enabling her, she's never going to get better. You have to stop handing over cash every Sunday for the cycle to break."

"Are you finished now Kellie?" Dad peers at me over the newspaper he's been pretending to read.

"No, I'm not finished, but I'll be silent if that's what you're really asking."

"Great, silent is perfect. Like your mother said, what we choose to do with our money is our business. If we want to pay for Leslie's rent and groceries, it's our choice and you need to stay out of it."

I couldn't believe what my father said, stunned I gathered my coat and went home. That was the last Sunday dinner we shared with Leslie.

Eight days later, standing beside Leslie's grave, I finally accepted the fact that it wasn't their fault.

That was the hardest day of my life. The finality of the situation hit me as my mother's sobs slowed to whimpers while we said our goodbyes for the last time. Rory cried and asked for her momma, insisting Mom or I hold her, which we both used to shield ourselves from the pain losing Leslie caused.

My parents were overwhelmed with grief and guilt. Months later, I still find Mom in tears while looking at old photographs of me and Leslie and try my best to comfort her.

"I'm sorry we never believed you, but…"

"It's not your fault Mom. Leslie kept you from seeing the side she knew would disappoint you. She wanted you to see the strong beautiful woman you raised us to be. You didn't do anything wrong."

"But if we had just trusted you and hadn't buried our heads, we might have been able to save her from…."

"Mom, Leslie was too lost in her addiction by that time, so you can't blame yourself. It was her choice to shoot up and ignore her baby. Now it's time to focus on Rory."

Usually these conversations ended with both of us in tears while reminiscing about the past.

I miss Leslie every day, but at times, I feel her death was a blessing. She's no longer struggling with addiction and Rory is safe with her grandparents and me.

Before the emergency custody order expired, I applied and received guardianship of Rory, knowing my parents would help as best they could. Mom and Dad are a godsend and love babysitting their only grandchild. They spoil her, but that's what grandparents do. She is also the only link they have to Leslie and it shows.

These old memories have distracted me long enough. It's time to quit procrastinating and finish getting ready for the party.

I can do this. I can go out with Gina and forget about the truck-load of responsibilities for just one night. I'm going to join my friend, have fun and let the old Kellie out of her dusty closet.

When I pull into Gina's complex, I see the limo is already parked and waiting.

Teetering on the spikey heels Gina insisted I wear is hard enough on level ground but scaling the five stairs to the front door might require a 911 call. Thank god for the sturdy handrails that help me climb safely to the entrance.

Gina pulls the door open before I get to the top step, thrusting a shot glass full of purple liquid toward me. It spills a little and I catch the strong odor of tequila. "Not for me thanks, not while I'm in these heels."

"Suit yourself." She tilts her head back and swallows the liquor in one gulp. I catch sight of what she is calling an outfit. A hot-pink strapless dress that barely covers her massive boobs. There is a high probability of her having a wardrobe malfunction tonight. As I suspected, she is wearing the bride to be sash.

"Kellie, you made it just in time, but you're two shots behind. Get inside and catch up, then we're out the door for my last night as a single woman." She steps to the side and sways a little, indicating she's had a few more than just two shots. I recognize a few of her cousins standing around the table with their own shots in hand.

"Come on. I'm getting married tomorrow and we need to celebrate."

What have I gotten myself into?

Deciding it won't kill me to have one shot with everyone before we leave for the bar, I reach for the glass with the least amount of alcohol in it and raise it to clink with Gina's. "Cheers!"

We all toss the tequila back, slamming the glass upside down on the table to prove we drank every drop. The burning sensation running down my throat feels foreign after months of not touching a drop of alcohol.

Gina holds the tequila bottle above her head like a trophy. "Who's for more shots."

If I let her continue at this pace, she's going to need to be poured into the limo. I guess it's time to clock in as maid of honor. "Let's check our makeup and head out to the limo. It's time to get your party started."

That was all Gina needed to change gears. She hustles to the back of her apartment, returning with her purse and thin shoulder wrap. "I think I have everything, Kel, are you ready?"

"As ready as I'll ever be." Thankfully, my mumble is barely audible and draws no response from Gina.

We link arms as we follow the other girls out the door. I struggle descending the stairs in these deathtrap heels, certain they'll be tossed to the side ten minutes into dancing. I'm not sure why I wore them. Oh yeah, I do, they look hot.

We reach the limo, but Gina turns back to her apartment calling over her shoulder, "Hang on, I forgot something."

I'm in awe watching her run in her six-inch *Jimmy Choo's*. That girl has skills.

Gina returns carrying a large gift bag in the shape of a cartoon penis. Great. Let the silly cock jokes begin.

She hands me my Maid of Honor sash. I try not to groan as I pull it over my head, letting it fall on my shoulder. Gina is still digging in the bag for more party favors, handing out plastic headbands with springy penises. Oh, but there's more. She hands each of us a novelty *Ring Pop*. I loved these candy rings when I was kid, pretending to be rich, showing off my huge hard candy ruby. Only this ring doesn't have a large candy jewel on top. Instead it has colorful candy penis.

We are meeting more ladies at the bar so there are enough supplies to go around. They went ahead of us to set up the reserved area and decorate, no doubt with more representations of the male member.

Kill me now.

5

LANCE

As I enter Heath's, I spot my buddies who have already commandeered our regular tables in the corner near the back wall. I make my way through the crowded bar and greet my friends. "Hey guys. Who are we still waiting on?"

One of the new recruits, Javier Valez, speaks up. "I think this is everyone."

Out of habit, my eyes scan the room. It's Friday night so I expected it would be busy. Looking around, I see many of the regulars but there are also a few faces I don't recognize.

"Cool. What are we playing tonight? Pool or darts?" We have a round robin style tournament each week. To enter, each player adds twenty dollars to the pot. The losing team delivers the cash to the local high school to help fund after school activities.

Sergeant Dean Williams speaks up. "Darts. You ready to get your ass handed to you?" He can't hide the bitterness in his voice. His losing streak over the past year set a new department record. I gotta hand it to him though. The guy is stubborn and won't give up. Each week, he switches partners hoping it will change his luck.

"Care to double the bet?" I should feel bad for goading

him but watching how riled up he becomes over a silly game is too much fun to pass up.

Our ultra-serious sergeant's eyes narrow and his face turns beet red as his obvious frustration bubbles to the surface. "You're on. Let me know when you and Paul are ready. I got a ringer. Rookie over there is going to surprise everyone." Javier's eyes widen when Dean points to him. I'm guessing the rookie isn't aware he's to be Dean's partner tonight.

"Yeah, yeah, I'll get Paul and let you know when we're ready."

I make my way down the row of tables to Paul. We have been best friends since meeting at the police academy and clicked immediately. Luckily for me, we're also on-duty partners. Over the years we've shared a lot and when he married his high school sweetheart, Jane, I was his best man.

As Paul's best friend, it was me who was there to pick up the pieces when Jane died two years ago after a short battle with an aggressive brain tumor. Paul has never been the same. There have been many times since Jane died that he calls me in the middle of the night needing to cry and let out the emotions he bottles up all day.

The anniversary of Jane's death is a month away which usually means I can expect an increase in those late-night calls. Hearing him talk about her through sobs is brutal. He misses her more as each day passes, but aside from listening to him pour his heart out, I have no other way to console him.

Paul is deep in conversation with the guys about the last call we were on before going off duty tonight.

I only catch the tail end of the story he's telling. "...then the jackass threw a punch forcing us to arrest both of them." Paul lifts his beer mug to take a drink, only to find it's already empty.

I pat Paul on his shoulder to get his attention. "I'm still

pissed at that asshole. Please tell me you finished that report so we don't have to do it tomorrow."

"Hey, Lance. About fucking time you got here." He kicks the chair out next to him. "Sit down."

I pull the chair over to the end of the table and sit. "Yeah, I took care of it before I left so you could get your beauty sleep. I need another beer." Paul stops the waitress, Cindy, as she passes by our table and orders two drafts.

Before the waitress turns away, I change my order. "Ah, no beer for me tonight. Can I get a sweet iced tea please, no lemon?"

"Sure, hun, are you the designated driver tonight? Remember DD's drink free."

"No, but I'm not in the mood for beer tonight."

"Gotcha, I'll be back in just a sec."

It's a busy night so I'm not expecting to see her back soon. Time to check in about Jane. I hate this part but what kind of partner would I be if I didn't? I lean in so only Paul can hear me. "You doing ok?"

He sits back in his chair and gives me a big toothy smile. "Everything's great with me. What about you? Did you call that badge bunny who slipped you her number?"

His abrupt change of subject only adds to my fear that he's slipping back into dark head space again. Paul knows what I'm asking and blew me off like he always does. Happy Paul on the outside, but completely heartbroken inside.

Rather than prod him for the truth, I answer his stupid question. He knows how annoyed I was at that time. "You're a dick. I was starving."

While eating lunch last week the waitress shamelessly flirted, leaned across the table and shoved her tits in my face while reaching to fill the sugar container. When I didn't pay her any attention, she resorted to sliding her phone number into my sandwich. Of course, I didn't notice until I took a bite. With paper sticking out of my mouth, Paul laughed his ass off

47

and told me to go chase after her. I threw the sandwich and phone number in the trash. This is another reason I like to bring my lunch with me from home.

"Mmmm, *my* sandwich was delicious. Too bad you didn't keep her number. I bet she would've given you something else to snack on." Paul doesn't try to hide his amusement, laughing loud enough to get some odd looks from the others in the bar. "Hey, I'm just messing with you partner. I hope someday you can find someone as great as Jane. I'm telling ya, meeting the love of your life changes you. It's like finding a piece of your soul that you didn't know was missing." Paul gets a far-off look. I imagine he's thinking of Jane again. When I think about the great love stories in history, Paul and Jane top the list.

"If only I could be so lucky to meet a woman as wonderful as Jane. She was one in a million." Finding someone like Jane to spend my life with, and who understands what it means to be part of my family of blue seems impossible.

Paul half stands from his chair while looking around the room. "Where's Cindy? They have her hopping again tonight. Heath really needs to hire some help and give his staff a break."

His change of subject clues me in that he doesn't want to talk about Jane right now.

"I agree, Heath works his waitress's too hard. It's no wonder the turnover of employees is so high. She's making her way over to us now."

As if on cue, our drinks are placed in front of us and I take a huge gulp of the sweet tea. Paul follows by chugging down the entire beer in one swig. With an exaggerated belch, he slams his mug on the table with such a loud thud, several people look in our direction. Cindy spins around and stares at Paul who gives her a sheepish grin. "Sorry darlin', I didn't mean to be so crude. I know you're swamped but can you bring me another beer on your next sweep through?"

Cindy giggles when Paul calls her darlin'. They've flirted for months but that's as far as it's gone so far. "Sure hun, just give me a minute to drop this tray off in the backroom. The bride-to-be is buying everyone shots and I can't seem to serve them fast enough." As she turns away, I swear she puts on a show with an extra wiggle to her hips just for Paul, only he doesn't react in the slightest.

"Please tell me you're finally going to ask Cindy on a date. You two have been circling each other for too long. Man up and ask the beautiful woman to dinner. Maybe you can catch a ride with her tonight." I'm hoping with my encouragement, Paul will pull himself out of this funk I watch him fall into each year.

The closer to the anniversary of Jane's death the more he withdraws into himself. But Jane is still a big part of his life. He works overtime to cover medical bills from Jane's illness. It isn't ideal, and while the sheriff's department provides us with good medical insurance, it never covers everything, especially the experimental treatments they tried in order to save her life. Paul claims to date women, but I know it's bull-shit. That's part of the problem. He has major issues trying to let go of Jane's ghost.

"That's not gonna happen man. After darts I'm going home and sleeping for days. I took next week off so I could take care of some things I've been putting off. Besides, she could have her pick of men in this place. Maybe you should ask her out."

"Cindy's great, but much too young for me. Seriously, how are you planning on getting home tonight?" I'm concerned but I know better than to push too far.

"Well, I planned on catching a ride with you but if you're not here when I'm ready to leave I'll call Uber. Now are we going to play darts or what?"

Paul's speech is slower than usual and he's beginning to slur his words. He must've been drinking more than beer

49

before I arrived. I'm worried he's trying to mask his emotions by drowning them in alcohol. Maybe I can ask Cindy to slow down when returning with his orders.

My chair scrapes on the hardwood floor as I stand. "Alright man. Give me a minute. I gotta take a piss. How 'bout you ease up on the alcohol and maybe you'll still be able to hit the bullseye?"

"Don't worry about me. I'll be fine. Hurry up."

As I walk away, I hear Paul continue his story about tonight's arrest.

After speaking with Cindy, I spot one of the deputies from our station, Jackson Locke. He's leaning on the bar talking to some sexy chick in a skintight black dress. If you could call it a dress. It didn't leave much to the imagination. The headband with the bouncing cocks is an instant turn-off and screams she is part of the bachelorette party. Exactly what I was trying to avoid.

"Jackson—ma'am. Sorry to interrupt."

Ever the gentleman, Jackson turns to introduce his friend. "Glad you made it, Lance. This is Melanie. She and her friends are here for a bachelorette party. I told her I'd help carry these trays to the back room."

"Nice to meet you, Lance. We could use an extra hand if you're not too busy. The bride to be and a few of the other ladies have over imbibed a touch. I thought water and sports drinks might help keep the party going a little longer and without it getting too out of hand. Maybe even make the ceremony tomorrow easier."

"Sure, I have time to help." We load up the trays as best we can, given our lack of experience as servers, and follow her lead.

This may be my only chance to speak with Jackson about

Paul. Not wanting to be overheard, I let Melanie get a few steps ahead and hopefully out of earshot before asking Jackson about my partner.

"Did you by chance see Paul?"

"Not yet," he replies. "I was about to grab a bite to eat when Melanie caught my attention. Why? What's up?"

"I may need your help. You know the anniversary of Jane's death isn't too far away."

"Yeah, I know."

"Paul's pretending everything's fine. When I mention talking to someone, he tells me he's great, better than ever and doesn't need any help."

Jackson may be the only one who can get through to Paul. He's one of the Springhill Sheriff's Department peer support leaders. Jackson volunteered a few years ago and has had extensive training relating to first responders and the specific situations they may encounter on and off the job. His dedication to helping us goes beyond what is expected, making himself available 24/7 for anyone who needs him.

One night over a few beers, I decided to ask what led him to becoming a peer support leader. I figured it was for the extra cash the training added to his paycheck, so his answer surprised me.

"Spill it Jackson. What's the real reason you spend so much time on peer support?"

He was silent for a moment, as if in deep thought about how he was going to answer me. When Jackson finally spoke, his words were powerful. "None of us are invincible, Lance. Sure, we are the ones who come to the aid of others, but what about when we need help? Who better to talk with than a fellow officer? I want to be that person who can be relied upon when one of my brothers or sisters needs me."

I let his word sink in, but had a feeling there was more to it, so I asked him to elaborate.

"Alright, I can see that, but for you it seems more personal than

just wanting to help others. There has to be more to this story. Why is being a peer support leader important to you and not just another opportunity for overtime pay?"

Jackson doesn't hesitate this time. *"Yeah, I guess you could say there's more to it. My decision isn't based on extra money because I donate what they would have paid me to the community women's shelter. The reason I do it is because of my own experience with peer support."* He leans back in his chair and continues. *"Before you were hired, I had an incident I couldn't shake. It was a domestic violence call that didn't end well. The father shot and killed his wife and two sons before we could get to the house. Flashbacks from that call kept me wide awake at night. It started with over the counter pills. They didn't help and only made me groggy the next day. A few months had gone by and one morning, after our group muster, Lieutenant Cartwright pulled me into his office to talk. You know that's never a good sign."* He chuckles nervously.

"Yeah, I've been called in to talk to Cartwright before. So, what did LT say?" I wasn't just shooting the shit with Jackson. I really want to know more about peer support and what services they provide.

"I walked into his office, preparing to be ripped to shreds over another report I didn't finish but instead found Cartwright and one of the peer support guys waiting on me. Long story short, they told me what they observed about changes in my behavior. I was quick to lose my temper over stupid shit, stopped hanging out after work and basically isolated myself from everyone. I didn't recognize it as a problem until they pointed it out. I'm not sure what direction my life would have gone without them. Now it's my turn to give back and help others." Jackson reaches for his mug, swallowing the remainder of his beer.

"Wow, I had no idea." I was stunned. Jackson is the guy who always has his shit together. Reports finished, uniform pressed and badge polished. The poster boy for how an officer should look and behave. I'd have never guessed there was a time he struggled emotionally.

"I'm not ashamed of my past. In fact, I don't keep it a secret. I've told my story before, when asked. I just don't go around publicizing it. I've been there myself, so if you ever need to talk, I'm here. No judgement."

That conversation was one I'll never forget. It's why I'm turning to Jackson for help with Paul now.

Jackson stops walking and turns giving me his full attention. "Alright, you know Paul better than anyone. If you say your partner needs help, we need to find a way to get it for him. What do you have in mind?"

"Maybe you can help me convince him to go to the upcoming peer meeting."

"I'll do my best, but you know how hardheaded he is."

"Yeah, he can be a stubborn ass on a good day. How about you meet me at his house tomorrow around 7:00am? Maybe if he wakes up with a massive hangover it will help us get our point across."

"Yeah, I can do that. You better bring lots of coffee. Now let's get these drinks handed out." Jackson rushes off. I'm assuming he's eager to find Melanie.

After months of trying to get Paul some support, I feel I'm finally getting somewhere. He's not going to like what Jackson and I have to say, but I won't leave until he listens this time.

I follow behind Jackson intending to go unnoticed, wanting to get started on the dart tournament. Instead I'm frozen in place, not believing what I see in front of me.

Holy Shit! I've been coming to Heath's for years, seen multiple bachelor and bachelorette parties, but this one is completely over the top. The room looks like a penis bomb exploded in it. Balloons, tablecloths, wall hangings, all sporting images of cocks of various shapes and sizes. I've never seen so many representations of the male member.

Off to my right, it looks like the ladies are playing a game of pin the tail on the donkey. Only instead it was pin the cock on the guy hanging on the wall with the porn-tache.

One of the ladies, a tall, loud-mouthed redhead, is spinning a short, plus sized woman, wearing a blindfold, around in circles. On the fifth turn, the redhead stops turning the woman and lines her up a few steps away from the wall. Unfortunately, she takes two steps, stumbles, and falls flat on her ass. The ladies surrounding her cackle like hens without bothering to help her up.

I'm still holding the heavy tray of glasses, wondering where to set them down when I notice a woman leaning against the wall at the back of the room. She isn't wild and rowdy like the other ladies, quite the opposite. There is something classy about her–the craziness isn't for her.

For some reason I'm drawn to her and can't stop staring. She's beautiful with dark shoulder length hair that shines under the lights twinkling around the room. Her black dress is sexy without revealing too much. It shows off her curves to perfection and leaves me wondering what she's hiding underneath the garment.

The mystery girl has my full attention and I don't notice the woman standing in front of me. It takes me a few seconds to realize who she is. My ex-girlfriend, Patricia, the last person I want to see. She catches me off guard when she reaches for my junk. With the full tray of drinks, I'm not able to push her hand away in time. She tapes one of the paper cocks to my zipper and shouts over her shoulder to the group of women staring in our direction. "I did it, now pay up bitches."

6

KELLIE

The party is still going strong and has taken a turn from playful to cringeworthy with the way some of these ladies are behaving. I say ladies only to be polite. I'm not a prude, and all for letting your hair down and having a few drinks but being so drunk you won't remember the next day is crazy.

It all started with the adult version of pin the tail on the donkey. Instead of the cute cartoon donkey with a missing tail, there is a naked man with large penis stickers. It quickly got out of hand when Gina's cousin, Trish, tried to tape a paper cock on the zipper of the guy carrying drinks. I don't know why she's even here after making such an ass of herself at the bridal shower last week.

Gina's aunts hosted a classic garden party at her parents' home. A multi-generation gathering of family and friends to celebrate another wedding. Over the past century, this historic house has seen more than one hundred weddings, bridal and baby showers.

I can understand why because it's the perfect setting. Over thirty acres, with a large patio surrounded by mature oak trees which provide shade as well as privacy. Situated in the center of the garden is an ivy-covered gazebo, simply decorated with climbing jasmine and twinkle lights. I could only dream of having my own special day in this picturesque location.

The elderly ladies in attendance were a hoot. Each one talking about the past and how gentlemen courted their future brides. I did my best to hold back my giggles when they offered advice on how the virgin bride should prepare for her wedding night.

It was all so different for their generation. No online dating and bars. Couples had to make an effort to find that special person. Old-fashioned courting sounds ideal for me, but men like that do not exist anymore.

We were asked to dress conservatively for this traditional, elegant, and sophisticated affair although Trish must not have received the memo. Her ruby red, strapless sundress was unsuitable attire for an occasion such as this.

Squeezing herself into an outfit at least three sizes too small, her boobs spilled over the top raising the eyebrows amongst the older guests. That wasn't the worst of it though. The slit up the side of the dress was so high her black lace underwear was just visible.

Shortly after lunch, Trish decided the champagne punch being served wasn't strong enough and pulled a bottle of vodka from her bag to kick things up. Her table of groupies began drinking with her, encouraging Trish's bad behavior.

Unfortunately, as Gina was opening gifts, Trish decided to shout out a few sexual positions Dirk and Gina could try after the wedding. "Don't forget the no missionary rule on your honeymoon! Save that ribbon so Dirk can tie you to the bed and…"

Gina's aunts quickly swooped Trish up and dragged her into the house before she could cause any more problems. The elderly ladies gasped, and a few expressed their disgust with Trish's display of rude and raunchy words.

Apparently, Trish is notorious for this type of behavior.

She's that family member who nobody wants to invite to events, yet they feel obligated to have her there. I'm guessing this is the only reason she's been invited to tonight's party.

I'd love to confront Trish about her paper cock performance but decide not to stoop to her level. However, as the maid of honor, and one of the only sober women here, I feel the need to apologize and make amends for Trish's embarrassing actions.

Leaving the dark corner I've been hiding in all night, I approach the man who Trish accosted earlier. At least the music has been turned down from the ear-splitting level it's been at for hours, so I won't need to shout to be heard.

As I get closer, a strange feeling of Deja vu clouds my mind as I get the feeling I've seen him before. I brush it off as just being another handsome muscular man in a crowded bar.

"I am so sorry. You'll have to forgive her. I'd like to say it's the alcohol talking but she's really just a classless bitch who acts like this regularly."

He doesn't respond, only stares, making me feel a little self-conscious. Do I have something on my face? I try my best to be discreet as I rub my nose before looking up into his eyes again. He's about six inches taller than me. If I'd kept my heels on, he wouldn't seem such a giant, but my aching feet won the war between sexy and comfort hours ago.

Finally, he breaks the silence between us, "No problem ma'am. Not the first time something like this has happened."

WTF? How is someone used to getting felt up at a bachelorette party. Maybe he enjoyed Trish's attention and I should introduce them before I leave.

Oh wait, I get it now. He must be the stripper the girls talked about ordering last week.

"Well the bride is over there wearing the toilet paper dress and the stage is all set up for you with a few chairs." I point over to the raised platform with the convenient stripper pole and bright lights. A few of the ladies have been practicing and falling on their asses, keeping me entertained. I especially enjoyed watching Trish hit the hard wood floor with a loud thud. Everyone froze thinking she had hurt herself before breaking into uncontrollable laughter. No doubt the epic crash will leave a mark and have Trish waking up tomorrow trying to figure out where that mystery bruise came from.

"I think you've made the wrong assumption, ma'am. I'm not the bride's entertainment. I'm helping Melanie. I met her at the bar with my buddy and saw she needed an extra hand with these drinks."

Too bad he's not the stripper. I might've grabbed a front row seat for his show. He's balancing the tray of glasses on one hand, using his shoulder to keep it from toppling over. The flex of his bicep has the sleeve of his black T-shirt stretched so tight I'm surprised it isn't busting the seams. His dark hair is cut short around the sides and is just a bit longer on the top. A very clean-cut gentleman, who is also sexy as sin.

Simply looking at this guy has me heating up from the inside out. If I had my way, he'd give me a private strip show. I'm not sure where these dirty thoughts are coming from. Perhaps getting out of the house and spending time with other adults has reminded my body that I'm a twenty-four-year-old single woman who hasn't had sex in a long time.

I should probably apologize for my confusion, only I can't seem to find my voice. My throat is dry, and my tongue is stuck to the roof of my mouth. I feel the perspiration melting my makeup and dab my face with a cocktail napkin from the table, praying I don't look a sweaty mess.

"Let me set this down. You look like you could use some water." As if the full tray of glasses was feather light, he expertly sets it on the high table beside us without spilling a drop.

Accepting the offered water glass, I take a long drink,

enjoying the contrast to the heat I feel running through my body.

"Thanks, that hits the spot." I lick away the drop of water sitting on my lower lip while letting my gaze drift over Mr. Sexy. Without conscious thought, X-rated images of the two of us invade my mind. "Mmmm, but I'd rather you hit my spot."

He raises an eyebrow, tips his head slightly to the side and gives me a cocky grin. "You're welcome for the water, but don't you think we should at least know each other's names before we start talking about hitting spots?"

FUCK! NO! I did not say that out loud. My brain and mouth need to get on the same page. *Think fast!* How am I going to cover up this faux pas? "Ah, wow, I don't know where that came from. That last shot must have gone straight to my head." My nervous giggle does nothing to cover up that lame excuse.

His grin fades, changing his face to almost expressionless. Relaxed jaw, closed lips but not pressed tight. "How much have you had to drink?"

Who is this guy? I don't owe him any explanation but answer him anyway. "Not that it's any of your business, I had a shot before leaving the house about four hours ago and a beer when we first got here. As the maid of honor, I also have the *honor* of being the bride's babysitter." I use annoying air quotes when I say honor. "Had I known this was one of my jobs, I may have told Gina I was out of town this weekend."

I must have given him the answer he was looking for as his smile returns. "I hope the others have a safe way to get home?"

A guy from the far corner of the bar stands up and shouts something in our direction about darts before walking to the game room.

It's then that I notice the other men with short hair

wearing dark T-shirts that barely cover their muscles. Classic cop attire and looks.

Now I understand this line of questioning. I can't fault him for wanting us to be safe. "The limo will fit most of us, and the rest have sober rides or *Uber*. Thanks for your concern, Officer…"

He extends his hand to shake mine in a business-like manner. "When I'm on duty it's Deputy Lance Malloy. Well I guess the deputy part never fully leaves, but please call me Lance. And you are…?"

The name Deputy Malloy echoes through my mind. *Could it really be him?* I think back to the best and worst day of my life. The day I lost my sister but rescued Rory. I try to match the images in my memory with the man standing in front of me. His hair is longer than I remember and without his uniform on it's hard to tell for sure.

"I'm Kellie. Kellie Bryant. It's nice to meet you, Lance."

Lance pauses, narrows his eyes, and blinks a few times as if to focus his vision. "Nice to meet you, Kellie. Wait, have we met before? Your name sounds familiar." I can see the cogs spinning in his head, like he's sifting through memories trying to place my name.

"Maybe. I think you were one of the officers who arrived the night my sister died, and I took custody of my niece, Rory." He doesn't say anything, so I continue my babbling. "I'm sure you don't remember since you see a lot of people in your job."

And then it happens. Lance's expression changes to what I think is recognition. The instant I see his wide grin and those dimples pop I have no doubt, this is my Deputy Malloy. The man who has invaded my dreams for months.

"As a matter of fact, I do remember that call and I'm sorry to hear about your sister. We were called to that apartment complex daily. I'm glad they finally demolished it. How is little Princess Rory doing?"

"Wow. I can't believe you remember. Rory is doing great. She still carries that bear you gave her. It's her favorite. She calls him Mr. Deputy and won't go anywhere without him."

"That's really great to hear. That was a tough night for both of you. We carry those stuffed bears for children to help sooth them after a traumatic incident. I'm glad Rory still loves her Mr. Deputy." Lance chuckles when saying the stuffed bear's name.

The drunk partygoers begin clapping and whooping it up. Lance stares past me and asks, "So tell me Kellie... why aren't you getting wild and crazy with the rest of the ladies?"

I peek over my shoulder to see what he is referring to and instantly regret it. Some things you just can't unsee. With everyone in a circle chanting her name, Trish begins twerking to the beat of Sir Mix-A-Lot's Baby Got Back. "Fun? You mean like that? Getting sloppy drunk, making a fool of myself and falling all over the place is not my idea of fun."

With a devilish grin, he leans in to whisper in my ear. I'm so busy piecing together what is happening right now that I almost miss his next words. "So, tell me Kellie. What is your idea of fun?"

Holy hell. My pussy clenches with every flirtatious word he whispers. Lance's hot breath next to my ear brings on a wave of goosebumps. On a deep inhale to calm myself, his cologne invades my senses. He smells just like I imagined he would. It reminds me of being outdoors on a sunny day. Fresh and with a hint of citrus. It's subtle, not overpowering the way some men wear it. I take in his masculine scent once more and fight the strong urge to lean in and rub on him like a cat in heat.

Remembering I have a rare night without Rory I decide to see where this might go. With an attempt to flirt back I reply, "I can think of a few fun things I'd like to do with you." The second the words come out of my mouth; I cringe. I must sound such a fool. It has been too long, and my flirting game is sorely out of practice.

It doesn't seem to deter Lance as he gently places his fingers on my chin and tips my head back. Looking into his gorgeous grey-blue eyes I am his. "Oh, really now. I'd love to hear more."

Speaking in full sentences is not an option. "Umm, maybe–umm, just forget what I said. I have to get home early...wedding stuff..."

The group of ladies behind me start cheering and screeching loudly when the real stripper, dressed in fireman attire, complete with a hose, steps up on stage. *Ugh, really?*

Lance clears his throat drawing my attention away from the stage and back to his sexy smile. "I need to meet my partner in the game room for darts. Come with me, it will be quick, and you can cheer me on. Unless you want to stick around and see Frank the Fireman flash his hose?"

"Oh no. I have no desire to see his hose, but I do need to check on the bride and can meet you over there." Gina should be entertained for the next hour, giving me time to get to know Lance and see where this night goes.

"I was hoping you'd say that. Don't take too long."

I'm treated to a wink and sweet smile before Lance turns to leave the party area. My eyes follow his gorgeous backside as he walks away from the craziness inside this room. Tonight just got interesting.

7

LANCE

My plan to grab a burger, play darts, and get home quickly have come to a complete halt. Not all calls stick with me, but Kellie's did. I tend to remember all incidents involving children, but watching Kellie take care of her niece brought on a wave of emotion I've been trained to ignore.

Keeping a professional distance when dealing with the worst times in someone's life keeps me neutral. Kellie's concern for both her sister and Rory wedged its way inside my heart and would pop up occasionally when in similar situations. I never expected to see her again but here we are, and I'd be stupid to let this opportunity slip by.

I've never been so instantly attracted to a woman before. I'm almost glad Patricia decided to pull her stunt. Without it, Kellie wouldn't have come over to apologize.

It didn't seem necessary to tell Kellie that Patricia is my ex. I can't believe she's changed her name to Trish again. When we dated, she told me she hated when people shortened her given name, insisting I call her Patricia.

I'm glad she walked away and didn't cause a scene. After our breakup she went a little crazy, stopping by the station before and after my shift. Even waiting outside my house until I finished. If she were a man, she would have been arrested for stalking, but I tried to give her a break. I finally threatened to get a restraining order after she broke into my house, got naked, and passed out drunk waiting for me in my bed. She's lucky she didn't get shot that night. The empty bottle of whiskey laying next to her prompted me to call her best friend Sara to pick her up instead of calling in the break-in. Sara promised to get her some help.

I see Paul walking in the direction of the game room and call out to him. "Wait up."

"Dude, where'd you go?" He isn't slurring as much as he was earlier but is still a little glassy eyed.

"Jackson needed a hand." I look over my shoulder, back to where Kellie is talking to one of the women waving dollar bills in the air.

"I see Frank's tonight's entertainment. That guy must make a killing doing these parties." Paul is looking past me to the woman fighting for the half naked stripper's attention.

"Why? Are you thinking about a side job?" I chuckle and step past Paul. Razzing each other comes naturally and is just another way we blow off steam.

Paul stops me with a hand on my shoulder. His face is dead serious. "Uh, that would be a hell no. Those ladies are crazy."

"I couldn't agree more." The thought of drawing out the game and missing out on getting to know Kellie has me trying to figure out a way to tell Paul without going into details. "Hey, I was just thinking, instead of screwing around and letting sarge and the rookie think they have a chance to win, how about we put 'em out of their misery quick."

A wicked smile spreads over Paul's face. He looks like the cat who ate the canary. "Who is she?"

This fucker knows me too well. There's no use denying it. I scrub my face before I admit why I want to finish the game fast and get on with the rest of my night. "Do you remember that call to the crack house apartment a few months back? The one where the aunt arrived before we got there and she had her niece, that sweet little girl named Rory."

"Yeah. You've talked about that incident more than once. What about it?" Paul knows how frustrated I get when children are involved and doesn't seem too surprised when I mention it.

"Well, do you remember me telling you if I'd met the aunt under different circumstances, I'd have asked her out?"

"How can I forget? You talk about that woman more than you probably realize. Are you saying she's here tonight?" Even though he hasn't a clue what Kellie looks like, he scans the room as if searching for her.

"Yeah she is. I bumped into her in the back room. She's part of the bachelorette party."

"Dude, that's great. Sounds like fate is playing matchmaker tonight. Do I get to meet this woman that's put you in such a great mood? I haven't seen that stupid grin on your face in a long time."

Hoping Paul will follow me, I walk back toward the game room. He does. "She's supposed to come back while we shoot darts. I'd much rather spend time getting to know her without everyone asking questions, which is why I'd like to get things started as soon as possible."

"No problemo partner. I got your back on this one. Anyone that can put a smile like that on your face is A-OK in my book. Let's go crush Sarge's hopes and dreams of success one more time. Then you can get back to work, loverboy."

Paul holds his arm out, blocking me. "Hey Lance. I just thought of something. Maybe she's the Juliet to your Romeo, the way Jane was for me. Probably more like Belle to your Beast but you know what I mean. Love at first sight kind of shit." His laughter and teasing reminds me of the old Paul, almost making me forget the dark cloud that was hanging over him earlier.

65

I don't reply, but continue on to the game room thinking about Paul's comparison to him and Jane. He always said the minute he saw her, there was never a doubt, she would be his forever. I think I finally understand what he's saying because there is something pulling me in Kellie's direction, and I have no plans to stop it.

We make such quick work of destroying the other team, Kellie never made it in to watch. The rookie wasn't bad but still no competition for Paul and me. Well more Paul if I'm honest. Even buzzed he throws darts better than anyone here.

Before we leave the game area, Paul stops me. "I'm going to take off but just want to say thanks for everything you've done for me over the years. I couldn't ask for a better partner and best friend."

I chuckle and shake my head. "What's up with the I love you man drunk talk? Are you really that wasted?"

"Nah, I stopped drinking right after you disappeared into the bachelorette party. No drunk talk, just letting you know I'm glad to have you as my best friend and partner. I've been lucky to have you on my side and yeah, I love you man." He punches my shoulder and pretends to shadow box with me before giving me an unexpected hug.

Okay. That's odd even for him. Maybe things are going better than I initially thought. I'm still checking in with him tomorrow. One good night doesn't mean things are all fine and dandy.

"Yeah, you are lucky to have me as your partner. Do you need me to drive you home?" I'm sure I can get him home and return before Kellie is done with the party.

He holds up his phone with the *Uber* app showing his ride is here. "I set up a ride already. Go get your girl. Oh, and hey, just a head's up. I saw Patricia around the bar earlier."

"Yeah, I saw her too. Thankfully, she didn't make a scene, but something tells me she is just waiting to pounce."

With a shake of his head, he drops his voice and speaks in a serious tone. He gives me the same warning he always does about my ex. He never liked her. "Just watch out for that woman. I don't trust her after all the shit she pulled."

I agree with him and am grateful knowing he's got my back. "I don't either. Thanks for looking out for me. I'll catch up with you later."

Before leaving, Paul says, "By the way, before I forget, I really hope this girl is the one you've been searching for. There's no better feeling than falling in love and knowing you have someone waiting on you when you get home after a shitty day at work. If she is the one, hold on tight and don't let her go." Paul's voice is thick with emotion and heartache.

Guilt fills me as I realize Paul will be walking into an empty house. "Are you sure you don't want me to drive you home?"

"I'm sure. Now, go find your Juliette."

With a dismissive wave over his shoulder, Paul heads out the front door and I go in search of the beauty I can't stop thinking about.

8

KELLIE

Before leaving the party room to find Lance, I grab my small purse from the table piled high with coats and other bags. Now to find Gina and make sure she'll be okay while I'm gone.

I'm still stunned at seeing the deputy I've envisioned as the perfect man for me. But what if he isn't the man I've built him up to be? He does appear nice and kind, but like most women, I've misjudged men in the past. Deciding to throw caution to the wind, I decide to get to know him better.

He's hot and it's been a long time since I've had these feelings or been on a date. Not that this is a date but getting to know him is a step in the right direction.

A loud squeal from across the room gets my attention. *Ah, there she is!* Gina's sitting on a wooden chair in the center of the stage getting ready for Fireman Frank and his magical hose. The music has kicked up a notch again, so I shout into her ear to be heard. "Are you gonna be good if I go out into the bar area. This music is giving me a migraine." It's just a little white lie and she won't remember most of this in the morning anyway.

Gina half stands and wraps her arms around my neck, almost pulling both of us to the floor. "But Kellie, it's my party. You can't leave."

I untangle myself and guide her safely back to the chair. "I'm not leaving. I'm just going over to the bar where it's a little quieter. I won't be far and once the stripper is done with his show, I'll come back in. Deal?"

"Okay, deal." She's nodding her head like a bobble head doll, causing her hair to fly into her face. It's too silly to stop myself from giggling.

"Whoa, girl. Slow down with the head bob before you make yourself sick. Have fun and I'll be back in just a bit." Before stepping off the stage, I tease her with the reminder we always used in college when heading out for a party. "Alright, don't get into too much trouble and make good choices."

Walking away from the stage, I'm startled when a hand touches my shoulder and forcefully spins me around. "Where the fuck are you going? Are you too good to be here with us?"

"What the hell?" My confusion turns to understanding when I see who stopped me. I should have guessed. Trish is standing in front of me looking like a wild woman.

"I said, where the fuck are you going?" This time I recognize how slurred Trish's words are, hinting at the amount of alcohol running through her system.

I barely know her yet she's acting like I'm her worst enemy. Maybe it's just drunk talk and the fact that Trish is a raging bitch but I'm tired of her and her crappy attitude. "Fuck you, Trish. It's none of your business what I'm doing."

She places her hand on her chest and with an exaggerated intake of breath, pretends to be offended by my foul words. "Fuck me?" Without missing a beat, her psychotic sounding laughter fills the air, reminding me of Heath Ledgers version of The Joker. This woman really is completely cuckoo.

Her cackling abruptly stops, and her eyes, now narrow slits, focus on me like she's trying to burn a hole through my body.

She leans closer and through gritted teeth hisses her next question. "Who the hell do you think you are?" She swipes the back of her hand across her mouth before staggering back a few steps.

It's hard to take her seriously when she looks like she does. I notice she just smeared most of her lip tint, leaving a bright red rim around her lips. It makes me think about the crazy *Batman* villain even more.

I'm done with this conversation and decide to end it right now. "Whatever, Trish. I don't know what your problem is, but I won't make a scene at Gina's party. Something you never seem to care about. Your family is even fed up with your behavior. You're a joke!"

Looking closer I see the smudged mascara under her lashes and streaks down her cheeks, making me think she's been crying. It almost makes me feel sorry for her, but not enough to stop me from throwing one last jab. "Oh, and you might want to go look at yourself in the bathroom mirror. You have a little something right here." I make a circle with my finger in front of my face hoping she gets the clue about the mess she's made of her makeup.

Trish's mouth gapes open and eyes widen. I may have gone too far with my insults. She spins around in a huff, storming off I assume to the bathroom. A couple of Trish's friends run across the room, calling her name.

Seeing the hurt in her eyes before she rushed away didn't give me the satisfaction I was seeking. In fact, it did the exact opposite. She obviously has a problem and me acting like a complete bitch made things worse.

A flashback hits me full force of my sister Leslie in a similarly intoxicated state. How did I not see it before? I'm ashamed of my behavior. How would I feel knowing someone treated Leslie this way?

When Gina gets home from her honeymoon, I'll mention what happened tonight and what my gut is telling me. I couldn't help my sister, but that doesn't mean I shouldn't try with Trish. She's a bitch, but if she's addicted to drugs or alcohol, she may need to know someone cares and is there to stand by her. That is if she's willing, because unlike Leslie, she must recognize it herself and want to change.

I blow out a breath of frustration knowing there's nothing I can do tonight. Hopefully, Trish won't endanger herself, and will stay safe until Gina and I can sit down and talk with her.

Scanning the room, I see Gina lying on the stage floor while Frank straddles her hips playing up to the crowd. Looks like she'll be busy for the next hour or so giving me some time to talk to Lance.

After a quick trip to the ladies' room, I walk over to meet Lance, but the game room is almost empty apart from a few guys shooting pool.

Turning back toward the bar, I run smack into a brick wall. A solid, muscular, delicious smelling wall. "Oof."

Two strong arms stop me from falling. "Steady there. I gotcha." I cling onto him. "Are you alright?"

Looking up, I see Lance grinning down at me. My heart thumps against my chest while my legs turn to jelly. Thank God he has hold of me or I'd be a heap on the floor.

My body reacts to Lance's touch with a wave of goosebumps. The temperature in the room seems to have risen and my stomach is full of butterflies. Needing to control my overactive hormones, I step back before answering him. Play it cool, I tell myself. "Yeah, I'm good. I didn't see anyone playing darts, so I assumed you left."

"I'm not going anywhere. Come on. I'll buy you a drink. How 'bout it?" His smile is impossible to say no to.

"Okay, but what happened to darts?" Lance places his hand on the small of my back, guiding me to an empty table.

"I told my partner there was a pretty lady I wanted to get to know a little better and he practically shot a perfect match just to get me back to you sooner."

"He sounds like the perfect wingman."

"Paul's a great guy. A hopeless romantic who thinks everyone should find the love of their life. He thinks fate has brought us together again. Part of me thinks he could be right."

"Fate, huh?" I'm not sure I believe in fate. Well I didn't until tonight. "I'm beginning to think you're a big flirt, Deputy Malloy."

"Me?" Why does he look so surprised?

"Tell me, do these lines work on all the ladies you meet?"

"I don't make a habit of this…"

"Are you sure?" I tease. He's got to be pulling my leg. I don't mean to appear cynical but talk of fate and finding the love of one's life isn't the typical, I want to get to know you chat I'm used to.

"Really Kellie, I know you probably won't believe me, but it's not a line. I rarely date and I've never actually believed in fate before tonight." His voice is matter of fact, and he sounds sincere.

Lance is the perfect gentleman. I'm impressed as he pulls out my chair. The men I've dated previously wouldn't know chivalry if it bit them on the ass. I've heard some women complain about a man doing such simple things for them, but not me. Yes, I'm capable of pulling my own chair out or opening a door, but there's nothing wrong with a man showing a woman respect.

It's sad to think these old-fashioned values are in danger of becoming extinct. Instead of taking a seat, Lance asks what I'd like to drink.

I don't plan on having more alcohol tonight but don't want to sound like a prude either. "What are you having?"

"Just sweet tea. I'm not drinking tonight."

Relieved we seem to be on the same page I smile up at him. "Sounds perfect. I'll have the same please."

"Hang on, I'll go to the bar. The waitress is swamped."

When Lance steps up to the bar to order our tea, I look around the crowded room. I can't remember the last time I was with this many adults without small kids running around everywhere. On the opposite side of the room I see several tables pulled together with what looks like more cops enjoying themselves. A few of the men have their arms draped across the backs of the women sitting closely beside them.

Lance returns with two iced teas and a huge basket overflowing with fries.

"I ordered these after finishing darts. Will you share them with me?"

"Yes, thank you. I'm starving and they look delicious." I reach for one but drop it quickly.

"Be careful, they just came out of the fryer." Lance brings my fingers to his lips… "Do you mind?"

"Uh, no." I'm not sure what I just agreed to but I'm willing to give him my trust, for now.

He gently kisses the tips to ease the pain.

My mind wanders, thinking of all the other places I'd love him to kiss.

Another brush of his lips over my fingers as Lance asks, "Does it still hurt?"

I gently pull my hand away and whisper, "No."

"My magic kisses always make things better." He winks.

"Hang on I'll be right back. I didn't have enough hands. Do you need anything else, Kellie?"

Do you mean something besides your lips covering my body in kisses?

"Well, you'll probably think this is weird, but can you grab mustard?"

Lance doesn't make a wise ass comment like I'm used to hearing from my friends about my odd request, only nods and says, "You got it."

He returns quickly with three small bowls, ketchup, mustard and mayonnaise.

Lance dips a large steak fry in the ketchup then swirls it through the mayo before popping it into his mouth and chewing deliberately. A yummy sound escapes as he closes his eyes and hums. Oh God, how did he just make eating a fry look so sexy.

I watch intently as he licks the salt from his fingers. The parts of my body that have been dormant for so long are screaming at me to play along.

Lance picks up another fry from the basket, dips it into the mustard and holds it up for me to take a bite. Having him feed me seems too intimate, so instead I take the fry from him and bite it in half.

"I've never tried fries with mustard." He dips one into the bright yellow condiment and gives it a try. Watching Lance eat shouldn't be a turn on, but it is. I hold back a groan when his tongue slides across his lower lip. All I can think of is where I want his tongue and how I would gladly return the favor. My turn to make a yummy noise only it's not for what I'm chewing.

Lance interrupts my fantasy and says, "I like it. You have good taste."

If he only knew my thoughts were about kissing and

licking him like a lollipop, he would really know how good my tastes are.

"I've always loved mustard, on everything. Rory hates it and says it burns her mouth. The last time she asked to try it on her hot dog, she jumped up from the table, flapping her hand in front of her face like she was putting out a fire on her tongue."

Lance chuckles and says, "I bet life with her is an adventure."

"You can say that again. Our morning was busy with appointments but spending the afternoon at the park and seeing how happy she is melts my heart. You wouldn't recognize her now. She's grown so much in the last six months." I stop myself from bragging about Rory. What single guy wants to talk about a toddler when hanging out at a bar? However, Lance surprises me once again when a genuine smile appears on his gorgeous face as I talk about my niece.

"I'm glad to hear she's doing well. It was hard to see and hear her cry that day." After a slight pause, Lance reaches out, taking my hand in his and entwines our fingers before resting them back on the table. "I remember a lot about that day and even told Paul I'd wished I could have met you somewhere else so I could get to know you. So maybe fate really is a thing just like Paul said."

"So, who is this man with all the answers when it comes to women? He must be fighting them off with a stick if he's half as good as you are with pickup lines." I feel a little guilty asking because this question is a test to see if Lance really is too good to be true. If he's looking for just a one-night stand, then I'm not interested. With the mistakes I've made in the past about men, I can't afford to waste time on a guy who I can't see a future with.

"Paul's my on-duty partner and my best friend. You can say he is a guru of sorts, and if he wanted a woman in his life, he'd have the pick of them, but he only has eyes for one, his wife Jane."

"I see…"

"Sadly, she lost her battle with cancer and I don't see Paul ever finding someone to fill her shoes."

"I know how he must feel. When you lose someone you love so deeply, it's what I think losing a limb must feel like. You know they are gone, but you still feel them with you all the time." Pulling my hand away from Lance's, I aimlessly pick at small bits of French fries in the basket. Our lighthearted small talk has taken a dark turn into the heartache and pain of losing someone you love.

"Is that how it feels for you, with your sister?"

If I look up, Lance will see the tears I'm holding back, so I simply nod my head.

Sliding his chair over beside me, Lance quietly whispers, "I'm sorry, I didn't mean to make you sad. Are you going to be okay?"

"I think so. Will you excuse me a moment? I think I should go check on Gina and get her home."

"Of course. Would you like me to come with you?" Lance stands and pulls out my chair.

"Are you sure you want to after the um… incident, if you know what I mean." I glance down at his zipper to make my point.

"I think I can handle a room full of drunk women without too much of a problem." He reaches for my hand and says, "Come on. Let's go break up the party and get you and your friends home safe."

Hand in hand, Lance and I walk into the party room. I'm glad to see the strip show is over and people are starting to leave. Fireman Frank is near the stage, stepping back into his leather pants while laughing and chatting with a few of the ladies. He seems friendly, like this is just a job and not an excuse to find another one-night stand or another notch for his bedpost.

I see Gina's cousin, Melanie, exiting the bathroom with the bride to be leaning on her for support. "Hey Mel. Is she going to be okay?"

Melanie's eye's lock on to our linked fingers. She looks up as if she has a question but doesn't ask. I'm sure she will grill me later for the intimate details. "Gina just tossed her cookies, so I'd say she's ready to go home. Dirk is going to kill me for letting her get this hammered."

Gina's speaks up, sounding better than I expected. "Ha, like he's not swimming in vodka right now with his buddies." In her drunken state she notices me standing in front of her. "Kellie, where'd you go, and who's the hottie?"

I try to pull my hand away from Lance, but he holds on and introduces himself. "Hi, Gina, I'm Lance Malloy. Congratulations on your upcoming wedding."

"Oh, Kellie, he's polite and cute. You don't have a plus-one, you should totally bring him to the wedding tomorrow. Right Mel?"

Oh, God. Shoot me now. Not only did Gina just out me for not having a date to her wedding, making me look like a loser, but she invited the guy I just met to be my date.

"Don't mind her, she's drunk and has no idea what she's talking about. Come on, lets gather your things and get you home." I pull out a chair for Gina before she falls over. "You take a seat while Melanie and I straighten up and get your presents into the limo."

I walk to the gift table and begin cleaning up the mess.

"Let me help you," he volunteers. "Where do these boxes go?" Lance is so close I can feel the warmth of his breath on my neck.

He has my body on full alert, and I need to get control before I do something stupid like ask him to the wedding just so I can see him again. A little distance right now should help.

"We need to load up the limo when it returns from taking the other guest's home. Do you mind checking out front to see if it's here yet?"

"Sure." Lance plants a kiss on my cheek and leaves the room.

Just when I think I might have a moment to collect my thoughts, Melanie playfully bumps my shoulder.

"So, why don't you invite him to the wedding? Gina's right, he's cute. You know Aunt Rachel won't mind."

"Seriously? I just met him. Well, we met once before. It's a long story, but he's the deputy from when I took custody of Rory."

Mel's eyes widen with shock. "Shut up! No way! I guess this really is a small town."

"So, you see why I can't invite him. It's weird."

She shrugs her shoulders and says, "Weird? Sure, but I choose to believe in fairytales. This is destiny."

Melanie gathers the paper tablecloth and used plates, tossing them in the trash while I search for a chair to stand on. We need to remove the wall decorations and clean up to get our deposit back for the room rental.

Whoever decided to hang penis's all over the room is going to get their ass kicked. Standing on tip toe, trying to reach an extra-large member, I feel the wobbly chair begin to slip out from under me. Just when I think I'm going to crash to the floor, Lance comes to my rescue, plucking me off the chair as if I were feather light.

"Here, let me get those down before you kill yourself." He sets me down on my feet. "I'll finish this, and you get your friend ready to leave. I can meet you outside with the boxes when I'm done." His tone is commanding and direct, but not in that asshole, I'm a dominant man so do as I say way. It makes me think back to how he controlled the scene when we first met six months ago.

"Thanks for coming to my rescue, Deputy." Feeling playful, I walk away from Lance, adding a little wiggle to my hips in case he's watching. After a few steps I peek over my shoulder and smile. Yep, he's watching.

Getting Gina home isn't going to be an easy task. Between Lance and I, we manage to get her into the limo without too much difficulty.

"Thanks for your help." I am relieved he's here. "I'm not sure I would have been able to get her in there by myself." I toss my purse onto the leather seat beside Gina.

"You're welcome."

Something inside me says it's time to take a chance on this thing called fate. I dive in headfirst and pray I'm not making a mistake. "Hey, so I was wondering. I know it's short notice and as my best friend so kindly pointed out, I don't have a date for the wedding tomorrow, and if you're not busy and wanted to come by and..." Recognizing my rambling I stop talking, wishing the ground would swallow me up.

With a crooked smirk he responds. "Kellie, are you asking me on a date?"

"I guess I was, but I take it back. I mean, who asks someone out on a first date to a wedding."

"No way. You can't just take it back. It doesn't work that way." Lance's teasing tone gives me the courage to ask again.

"Deputy Malloy, would you like to be my plus-one at Gina's wedding tomorrow?"

"I'm glad you asked, because there was no way I was ready to let you get away tonight without setting up a date to see you again." He stops speaking abruptly as if he remembers something. "Shit. I'm meeting Paul tomorrow. What time is the wedding?"

"It starts at 3pm, but don't change your plans. I know this is last minute."

"Oh, you can't get rid of me that easy. I'll be done by then and can meet you there. What's your number?"

Rattling off the digits, Lance enters my number in his phone.

"I sent you a message so you have my number. Can you text me later with the address of the wedding venue?"

"Sure, but I really should probably get Gina home now." Excitement takes a tight hold. I will see him again. "Thank you for helping get her into the car." I lean down to peek into the limo and see Gina has fallen asleep.

"No problem. I'm glad I could help. I'd like to kiss you goodnight if that's ok?" I love how he isn't aggressive and respects me enough to ask.

"You're a rare breed, Deputy. I thought gentlemen like you were extinct."

"Not extinct, just on the endangered list. So, is that a yes?" His tongue sweeps over his bottom lip giving me a small glimpse of what he's offering.

Without a second thought I nod and step closer to him. "I'd love a kiss goodnight."

Lance tucks my hair behind my ears and cups my cheeks, tilting my face up to his. I'm twisted in knots. I need him to hurry up and kiss me, yet I want him to slow down so I can savor this perfect moment.

Finally, I feel a soft brush of his lips against mine. It's a magical kiss, just like the kind I imagine the prince gave the sleeping princess to wake her from her slumber.

This fantasy I've been dreaming of for six months has the potential to break my heart, but I can't help thinking Lance could make it come true.

"Good night, Kellie. I'll see you tomorrow." He holds the door and guides me inside, waiting until I get settled before closing it softly.

As the driver starts the car, I turn to see Lance disappear into the bar. I'm lost for words, trying to grasp tonight's turn of events. Hours ago, I did everything I could to get out of the bachelorette party and now, fate plays its hand and pushes me into the path of the man I've been dreaming of for six months. It's crazy! He's the man I hoped he would be.

Before we pull out of the parking lot, Gina falls into me, her head on my shoulder. I sit her upright and reach across for her seat belt. "Come on, Gina. Help me get the buckle snapped."

Half awake, Gina tries to help but her fumbling hands make the task harder than it needs to be. Time to change tactics. Maybe playing the silly game I use to buckle Rory into her car seat will work. "Okay, Gina let's try this. Raise your hands above your head. Good girl. Hold them up there until…" *CLICK*

Whew. I get it now. Drunk adults really are like toddlers. "Okay, you can put your arms down now."

"I can't believe it, Kel, I'm getting married. Thank you for being my friend and helping me tonight. I love you, Kellie. I couldn't do this without you." Her words trail off as she finally drifts off and snores. The sloppy smile pasted on her face would be cute if I weren't thinking ahead to how I was going to drag her up those stairs without breaking both our necks.

Our drive back to Gina's apartment was short. I nudge her with my shoulder before unbuckling myself then her. "Come on. Get up. We're home." She wakes up enough to walk up the stairs on her own.

After helping Gina out of her dress, she flops onto the bed. I drag her into place then pull the covers of her queen-sized bed over her. She's out cold before I return with the aspirin I insisted she take before falling asleep. I set the water and pills beside the bed. Maybe if she wakes up, she'll remember and take them.

Running back through the events from tonight, regret takes a hold of me. I can't believe I met Deputy Malloy. Even more startling, I can't believe I asked him to come to the wedding.

If I weren't so tired, I would be in the middle of a full-blown anxiety attack. Thankfully, my exhaustion is keeping my nerves at bay and I will worry about it tomorrow, or since it's after 3am, today.

9

LANCE

After helping Kellie bundle the inebriated bride-to-be into the back of the limo last night, I decided to head home myself. Unfortunately, I only get a few hours of sleep. With thoughts of Kellie running through my mind and worrying about Paul, I tossed and turned.

Paul was acting odd and totally different from the guy grieving the loss of his beloved wife. He was almost cheerful and totally out of character. Maybe I'm overthinking it. He probably has a girl on the side who means more than just a quick lay.

He can never replace Jane, but I'd like to see him happy again. Hell, I'd like a slice of happiness myself, which brings my thoughts back to Kellie.

Although our time together last night was short, I feel a connection I can't explain. At this point I don't care what cosmic entity may or may not have brought us together. The word kismet springs to mind. I'm not saying I believe in it, but there must be a reason for our meeting again the way we have.

I think back to last night. The way our bodies leaned toward one another told me the attraction between us is not one sided. Excitement at seeing Kellie catches me unaware, but I still plan to take it slow.

I've screwed up so many times jumping in with both feet, but this is different. I want serious, but we must get to know one another first. With Kellie comes Princess Rory, the adorable little girl who is the most important part of her life. They come as a package deal and I won't do anything to upset their world.

Getting to know her without interference from my job won't be easy, but I'm willing to give it my best shot. The biggest concern is Rory. She needs consistency and the last thing I want to do is confuse her, so I had better work out my intentions before we get too far down the track.

It's easy to forget there is a life to be lived outside of police work. Seeing Paul lose Jane makes me realize how precious time is. Something tells me it is now or never.

I'm a little nervous about our date tonight, but I can't focus on her right now or I won't get through what needs to be sorted this morning. It seems she's not that easy to forget about. I wonder about her dress. What will it look like? Will she cry at the wedding? Will she wear her hair up or down? Does she like to dance? All the answers to the many questions will have to wait until I finish with Paul's intervention.

It's 7:00 AM and I'm sitting outside Paul's house waiting for Jackson to arrive.

Although I feel this intervention is needed, and long over-due, I'm not sure how Paul will take our interference. But I'm not doing it alone. Having Jackson here to support me is important. Not because we're ganging up on Paul, but because he needs to know we all care about him and that we're ready to help in any way we can.

I type a quick text to Kellie.

· · ·

Me: Good Morning Beautiful. I hope I didn't wake you. Don't forget to send me the address to the venue. I'll be there as soon as my meeting with Paul is finished. I can't wait to see you again.

I hit send just as Jackson parks his truck behind mine.

He casually strolls over to my door, tapping on the window to get my attention. "Good morning, sunshine. You gonna sit in your truck all day or are we going to do this?" Jackson has a smile on his face. He's always happy in the morning.

"Fuck you and your cheery self." I climb out of my truck and reach into the back seat for the tray of coffee I picked up for everyone.

I wish I were in the mood to smile. Years of shift changes have screwed with my internal clock. To say I hate waking up before noon is an understatement.

"Aww, whats the matter, Lance? Did you get rejected by the woman I saw you with last night? I thought for sure you'd seal the deal and go home with her."

"You're an asshole, do you know that?"

"Touchy this morning…"

"No, I did not go home with Kellie because she was responsible for getting her friend home." Why am I bothering to explain this? "But for your information, I'm seeing her later today. Now, can we get a move on?"

My thoughts return to last night and how good Kellie felt in my arms. To the kiss I can't get out of my head. I wanted to grab and devour this beautiful woman standing in front of me, claim her and never let go, but once our lips touched, I realized slow but steady was the way to go.

"Yo, man! What was that? You looked a thousand miles away." His smirk says he knows the answer and is just trying to get a rise out of me.

Ignoring his question, I hand Jackson his coffee and take a drink from mine. "Let's get inside and see what shape Paul's in. I bet his ass is still in bed."

Paul's house is a single-story ranch style house with a wraparound porch. He and Jane loved to sit outside on their large rocking chairs and gaze at the stars. Once Jane was gone, Paul threw the chairs out with the trash. He said seeing them every day, and the memories attached to them, was too hard for him to handle.

I ring the doorbell three times. He must still be sleeping because I don't hear any movement inside. I check to see if the door is unlocked but as I suspected, it's not.

After ringing the bell again and no response, I change tactics, pounding on the center of the door in the same way I do when serving a search warrant.

BAM! BAM! BAM!

"Hey Paul! Get out here. We need to talk." My words are brisk and loud.

"Jackson, can you go around back and see if his truck is here? Maybe he woke up early and went to the store or something."

"You could be right, hang on." Jackson steps off the porch and walks to the rear of the house. I lean against the railing, grab my phone, and dial Paul's number but it goes straight to voicemail.

The crunch of Jackson's boots on the gravel walkway gets my attention. "His truck is there. Could he have walked somewhere?" He shields his eyes and peers into the front windows.

"I doubt it. I didn't think he was that drunk, but he must be passed out cold." Maybe this is not the right time. "We're going to have to drag him out of bed and throw him into a cold shower to get him to wake up and hear what we have to say." I use the side of my closed hand like a hammer to announce our presence at the door again.

BAM! BAM! BAM! BAM!

"Paul. God damn it, get up. We need to talk now."

Jackson is behind me, "No way he didn't hear that. What do you want to do?"

His question hangs in the air while I rack my brain for a plan. There's no way I'm walking away without finding out what's going on with Paul. I rub the back of my neck, the sweat coating my hand.

Something isn't right. "Fuck it. I'll pay for a new door. You ready?"

With a nod of affirmation, Jackson silently gives me the signal to kick in the door.

Getting into position, I step forward, raise my leg and kick with the heel of my boot beside the doorknob. The wood frame only cracks, requiring a second heel strike to dislodge the deadbolt.

The second kick does the job as the frame gives way. I use my shoulder to push the door open and look around before entering. Nothing in his front room seems out of sorts.

"Paul. Hey Paul! Get up you lazy asshole."

"Lance, maybe he's in there." Jackson uses his head to point towards Paul's office where a light is shining from under the door. If he's in there, he should have heard all the commotion.

"Paul. Are you in here?" The door isn't closed fully, allowing me to push it open. The unmistakable metallic odor hits me before I see Paul slumped forward over his desk, his head lying in a pool of blood.

"Fuck! Jackson, call it in."

"On it. I'll put it on speaker."

"911, what's your emergency?"

"This is Deputy Jackson Locke of the Springhill Sheriff's Department. 11-99, officer down. Head wound. Apparent suicide. 504 Archer St. Starting CPR."

Jackson is speaking to the dispatcher, but I focus on Paul and tune out. I don't hear their words.

A buzz of white noise fills my head and time stands still.

The sun's rays shine through the window like a spotlight on the gruesome scene before me. Looking around the room, the thundering heartbeat in my ears accelerates along with my breathing.

Blood spatters dot the white walls behind Paul.

I look up at the picture on that same wall. It's covered in blood spatters too. My heart sinks at the grizzly sight that now leaves a shadow on Paul and Jane's wedding day. The happy couple are standing at the church alter immediately after pledging their lives to each other. Jane looks beautiful and angelic in her white dress. I focus on Paul's smile, something missing from his life since losing Jane and wonder when he last felt genuinely happy.

Lined up under the windowsill are the boxes I helped Paul pack in the months following Jane's funeral. They are filled with pictures and other keepsakes he wanted to throw in the trash, but I was able to convince him to keep in storage.

As we packed, Paul shared stories about each item and by the time we'd sealed up the memories, we were both drunk from the bottle of expensive brandy we'd finished. It felt like closure at the time. I had no idea he'd opened the boxes again.

Laying on the desk beside Paul are three pieces I knew he treasured. Movie ticket stubs from their first date, the letter Jane wrote to Paul when he graduated from the academy, and the last picture taken of Jane before she entered the hospice.

My chest tightens when I think about Paul sifting through his past alone and how helpless he must have felt.

My cry of anguish is blocked by the lump in my throat. I'm frozen in place, gasping for air just as I imagine Paul did seconds after pulling the trigger.

"Lance! Fuck, Lance!" Jackson's shouting brings me back

into the moment and what I need to do. "Get Paul on the floor."

Lifting Paul's limp body out of the chair, I lower him to the floor and begin chest compressions while Jackson uses his jacket to apply pressure to his head wound.

My heart bangs in my chest. "Come on, Paul. Not like this, you asshole. Don't you dare die on me." A mix of sweat and tears pour down my cheeks while kneeling above my partner's limp, lifeless body.

I pause compressions and place my fingers on Paul's carotid artery to check for a pulse but feel nothing.

"Open your eyes and talk to me, Paul, for God's sake."

"Lance, come on, let me take over." It isn't a request. "Go outside and wait for the EMT's to arrive." He has already started working on Paul as I rush toward the door.

Hearing the sirens, I hurry outside to where the paramedics and several Sheriff's Department vehicles have parked. I feel numb and force the words out of my mouth. "In here. My partner, Paul..." I take a deep breath. "...he's shot himself." Even saying the words out loud churn my stomach. I taste bile in the back of my throat and swallow it back down.

Sergeant Williams stops me as I follow the paramedics. "Stay outside, Lance and let them do their job."

"Fuck you, Sarge. I have to help him. He needs me.... I need my friend..."

It's at that moment I cease to be Deputy Malloy and become Lance, the man whose best friend shot himself.

We have years of history between us. It can't end like this. This isn't how I want to say goodbye to him. I say a silent prayer to anybody who might be listening and beg for his life, for just one more chance to fix him. He might not realize, but I need him and always will.

Paul has pulled me out of the shit many times, the only man who knows how close I came to dropping out of the academy.

Fear of failing and not living up to what I thought were my dad's expectations held me back. After a brutal reprimand from the drill instructor because of another screw up I'd made that day, Paul found me in a drunken stupor writing my letter of resignation.

"Lance, pull your head out of your ass, keep your fucking mouth shut, and listen." Paul snatches the paper I'd been scribbling on and tears it in half.

"Fine. I'll just sit here and finish this bottle while you point out my mistakes too. Let's hear 'em." I tip the bottle of Jack Daniels back without caring how wasted I get.

"I said shut the fuck up." Paul pauses as if he's daring me to speak up. I keep quiet as he continues berating me. "Listen to me. You're trying to win a race against a man who's not even running. You've built your father up into some untouchable perfect hero and guess what? Nobody is perfect. We're all flawed. You, me, and yes, even your dad. The legendary Captain David Malloy makes mistakes." He allows his words to sink in. "Has your dad ever said he's not proud of you?"

"No, but It's not like I can tell him I'm failing out of the academy, so I've been avoiding him."

"You really are an idiot." Paul shakes his head and laughs.

I don't see what is humorous right now. "Fuck you, Paul. You don't know what it's like to be compared to someone and know you'll never be good enough."

"Do you really think everyone is comparing you to your dad?"

"Isn't it obvious?"

"What's obvious is how much of a leader you could be. Do you know why the instructors are harder on you? It's because you can sit at the top of the class but you're so busy competing with your dad you've lost sight of who you are. The sooner you get that through your head the sooner you'll be ready to move forward and find out who Deputy Lance Malloy is."

"But how do I do that?"

"I'll tell you this once, but will deny it if ever asked, so clean your ears out and stop wallowing in self pity."

"I'm not wallowing."

"If it wasn't for you, I would have dropped out months ago." It's Paul's turn to tip the bottle of Jack Daniels back.

"What the fuck are you talking about?"

"You've been living in your dad's shadow and in a way, I'm stuck in yours."

"You're not making any sense at all."

"Hear me out. We aren't as different as you may think. I want to be as good as you and always have. I saw you on day one of training and told myself he's the one to beat for class leader. Your eyes held a fire that told us you were the best. You lead by example, setting the pace for everyone to follow. Everyday you push me to be better and try harder just by standing by my side. I don't have to ask for your help, you're there because that's who you are."

"That's just what friends do for each other. It's nothing special."

"Okay then. Remember that day you helped me through the obstacle course when I was ready to give up? That fucking wall kicked my ass, but you stayed behind to help me even though it meant you'd have to run the course again next week. You failed the course but what I and everyone else saw was a man helping a friend in his weakest moment. It was then I knew it wasn't a competition between us and every officer there would be lucky to have you as their partner."

Paul silently sat on the bar stool beside me and allowed his words to sink into my thick skull. I had no idea he was competing with me just as I was my dad.

"Lance, stop thinking so hard. Your dad is a great officer and father, but you need to set your own path. Be your own man. Step out of his shadow and finish the academy strong. That saying your dad has about the weight of the badge and needing help to carry it is dead on. You should call him. I bet he's ready to help you balance some of the weight you've been trying to carry alone."

"You're right. Thank you for not giving up on me."

"Lance, I'd never give up on my brother. And by the way, I already put in a memo requesting to be your partner. I'll always have your back."

Only I didn't have his back this time. Guilt that I failed Paul has me doubled over, hands on my knees while the contents of my stomach spill out onto the grass.

I'd attended more crime scenes than I care to remember but this is one I would never forget. Deep down I knew Paul had killed himself the moment he didn't come to the door. Hope faded at discovering his lifeless body.

"Lance, let's get you cleaned up." Sarge pours a cleaning solution allowing me to wash Paul's blood from my hands then offers me a bottle of water I use to rinse my mouth.

I wipe my face with my handkerchief and try to make sense of everything.

"Why didn't I listen to my instincts?"

"Don't go there, Lance." Sarge is firm and in control as always.

"If I'd just gone home with Paul last night, I could have talked him out of it."

"You would have delayed the inevitable, that's all."

"You don't know that." I was trying to rationalize an action I could never comprehend. "Paul listens to me." I refuse to accept what Sarge is telling me as truth.

"Lance, take Paul out of this scenario and tell me, how many times have you seen this?"

"Too many times…"

"Exactly." His hand gripped my shoulder. "Once a person makes the decision to end their life, there is little anybody can do to change the outcome."

"I should have seen the signs. He was too upbeat last night."

"Because he knew his pain was almost at an end, Lance."

"I thought it was just stupid drunk talk and now I know he was trying to say goodbye."

"Paul loved you like a brother, you know that."

Tears filled my eyes. "What am I gonna do without him, Sarge?"

"Let's worry about one thing at a time. Right now, we need to get Paul to the hospital. Okay?"

The paramedics rush Paul out the door and into the waiting ambulance. My feet feel like they are entombed in cement, rendering me unable to move.

Jackson approaches.

"Come on, buddy, let's go." He guides me to Sergeant Williams' car.

I slump into the seat. The wail of sirens from multiple vehicles is deafening. Words fail me as my eyes fix on the flashing lights of the ambulance speeding away from the scene.

Minutes later we arrive at the hospital. Not waiting for Sarge to come to a complete stop, I scramble from the backseat, slamming the heavy door behind me.

"Fucking open!" Growling my frustration about how slow the automatic doors are opening, I force my body through the small space and run to the front desk with Jackson following close behind me.

Recognizing the head nurse at the intake station, I stand in front of the door that leads to the secure area of the ER. "Hey, Vince, can you buzz us through?"

He must have been alerted to our arrival and presses the security button, unlocking the solid door. "Of course, deputy, they just brought your partner in. I'll have someone take you back to the waiting area and a doctor will be in to talk to you soon."

A nurse meets us on the other side of the door and escorts us to a room at the end of the hall near the elevators. "Please wait in here and a doctor will be in to see you as soon as they have any information."

It's not lost on me that this is the same room we use when waiting to speak with a victim or witness. I've been in here many times imagining how helpless a relative would feel when stuck in this room waiting for news. Now it's my turn to experience that empty feeling of dread.

Jackson pulls out one of the hard-plastic chairs from under the round table in the center of the room. "Lance, sit down. I'll see what I can find out. Sarge will be here in a minute."

Following his direction, I rest my elbows on the table. Holding my head in my hands, I try to figure out where I went wrong. Questioning what I could have done differently. What signs I might have missed and why I didn't insist Paul get help sooner.

I hear the thud of Jackson's boot steps on the linoleum tiles as he walks out of the room and takes a left up the corridor toward the nurses' station. Beeping monitors, hushed voices about patient care and urgent commands fill the halls. Not caring who might hear, I break down, adding my sobs of anguish to the mix.

Experience tells me there is no way Paul is alive. But until I hear those words for myself, I will hang on to that tiny sliver of hope.

"Lance." A woman's voice I recognize cuts through the silence in the room.

"Patricia. What are you doing here?"

"I heard and..." She sits in the chair next to me. "...I want to be here for you."

With her hand outstretched to mine, I accept her kind gesture of comfort, while we wait for news.

Without me noticing, the room slowly fills with men and women in uniform. Off duty officers line the walls and find any available space. Standing together, this family of blue, we wait in silence.

Patricia leans close and whispers, "Would you like me to get you something from the cafeteria?"

"No, thanks." I couldn't stomach food or drink right now, but I do wonder how she knew about Paul? Her turning up here is unexpected.

"I'll get you something anyway."

A cellophane wrapped sandwich and paper cup filled with vending machine coffee is set in front of me. "Thanks, Patricia." I take a cautious sip and cringe. This black sludge should never be called coffee.

After what felt like hours, a doctor steps into the eerily quiet room. I jump to my feet. "How's Paul?"

"I'm sorry, Deputy, there was nothing we could do to save him."

The room spins.

I look about and note the shock on my colleagues faces. They are stunned into silence by the devastating news.

Patricia stands beside me and reaches for my hand. I pull away before our fingers link. Paul would be furious she is here in the first place.

"Thank you for being here, but I think you should go home."

"I'm so sorry about Paul. I just didn't want you to be alone." I see hurt in her eyes but at this moment, all I can feel is the anger for how I failed Paul. I remember him warning me about her and won't disrespect his memory by allowing her to stay. So, for now, she needs to go.

I turn my back to Patricia in hopes she understands I'm done talking and she needs to leave now.

When I turn back to look around the room, Patricia is gone. My colleagues are doing their best to comfort one another. Their mouths are moving but their words are a garbled mess because the voice inside my head shouts loudest.

Paul killed himself because you did nothing to stop him. Your partner is dead. You failed him.

I feel suffocated by the conversations going on around me. The words are meant to provide comfort but listening to everyone talk about what a great guy Paul was and how they'll miss him is too much, too soon. The need to escape overwhelms me and I shoulder past everyone in my rush to reach the hall.

"Lance, come on man. Let me help." I should have known Jackson would be the one to follow me.

"I need to get out of here."

"Alright, I'll drive you home, but before we go, the doctor asked if you'd like to see Paul.

How am I going to say goodbye to him? "I'm not sure…"

"They've cleaned him up." He gripped my shoulder. "I thought you'd want a few moments alone before they move him."

Do I want to see him? Can I handle it?

Seeing Paul's body will be painful, but I know I will regret not saying goodbye to him privately.

"I need to see him, but can we do it now before I change my mind?" The emotions I'm fighting to keep inside need to be released and I'd prefer to do it away from here.

"Let me speak to the guys then I'll come with you and wait outside while you see Paul."

"Thanks, Jackson."

"Will you be okay for a minute?"

"Yeah."

From where I'm standing, I can hear Jackson's words. They're meant to bring comfort, but for me, nothing will take away this pain I feel right now.

"We're all hurting. Paul's death is still too raw to process and I implore you to lean on each other for comfort. The other peer leaders and I will be available to you 24/7. Nobody is in this alone."

There are several voices who respond, "Yes sir."

Jackson continues. "Before I leave, I'd like to say a few words for our fallen brother." There is a slight pause. "Deputy Paul Lancaster. We thank you for your service and friendship. May you find the peace you've been searching for. Blessed are the peace makers as they are the children of God. Rest in peace brother, we have the watch from here." Another pause. "Now, if you would please bow your heads while we have a moment of silence."

I am escorted into a pale-yellow room. There are no pictures on the walls, nothing but a sterile space.

I can feel the echoes from the many last goodbyes this room has undoubtably seen.

Paul's lifeless body is covered from the neck down by a white sheet.

The staff have cleaned him up as best they can, but apart from the pale color of his skin he could be sleeping.

Biting the inside of my cheek and holding my breath does nothing to halt the flow of my tears.

Pulling the stool over to the bed, I sit, then move the sheet just enough to hold Paul's hand. Lifting his palm to my cheek, he is cold to the touch, another reminder Paul won't be coming home.

"Why did you do it, Paul?" I hear anger in my voice. "Why didn't you trust me to help you?" I am asking questions that will never be answered. "How could I not know things were this bad?" Tears fall down my cheeks. "I'd have laid down my life for you if you'd only asked me."

Looking up to the bright lights, I hold my breath and squeeze my eyes tight shut, trying to regain a semblance of control.

"You're more than my partner, Paul. More than my best

friend. You're my brother. Like you always say, we don't share the same DNA, but we share a bond stronger than blood." My words come out as sobs. "Even in death, our friendship will never end. You were my strength when I needed it, I only wish I could have been yours too. No other partner will ever be good enough to fill your shoes."

I kiss Paul's hand, then carefully set it down back under the sheet. Straightening the covers over his body, I close my eyes once more as memories of the good times flood back to me.

Standing above my partner's body, I bend down and place my lips on his forehead. Then I stand straight, proud, ready to say my goodbye to one of the best men I ever knew. Tears cloud my vision, but I had to speak my truth before leaving him.

"Paul, wherever you are, I hope Jane is with you, and together you find peace for eternity. I'll never forget you. I love you, brother."

I never spoke a word during the journey home. Drowning in grief, idle chit chat was something I couldn't give.

"Lance, are you ready to go inside?"

So lost in my thoughts, I didn't realize we were parked outside my house.

"Yeah, okay. You don't have to stay though. I'm good."

"I'm staying, Lance. Now let's go." Jackson's stern voice says, don't argue because you won't win.

"Thanks." Deep down I do need the company.

Dragging my weary body out of the truck and into the house is a chore. The weight of the world is sitting on my shoulders, pulling me down into my own personal hell.

"Lance? What do you want for lunch? I know you didn't

eat any of the takeout that was brought in at the hospital, or whatever Patricia bought for you."

"I don't want to fucking eat. I'm not going to argue about you being here, but don't treat me with kid gloves." Spewing my anger at Jackson isn't fair, but right now I don't give a fuck.

Rubbing the back of my neck, I look up to the ceiling and curse.

"Shit." I really do give a fuck, and this isn't me.

Anger, hurt, and confusion crushes me. My usual calm is replaced by chaos.

"Jackson, I'm sorry and I'm grateful you're here. Look, I need to call my parents then I'm going to take a shower. I'll eat anything. Thanks for sticking around."

"You don't have to be sorry. You're not alone, Lance. Your family is here to support you. I'll have some food ready when you get out."

Like a zombie, I walk away and allow his words to sink in. I know everyone in the Sheriff's department is hurting, but right now I can only focus on my own grief.

Searching for the right words; how do I tell my parents about Paul's death without breaking down? I decide against holding back my emotions because these two people are the ones I never have to hide my true self from.

My mind is so messed up, I forget Mom and Dad are in Italy—a trip they have been planning for years. When my mom picks up, I swallow the lump in my throat.

"Can you put the phone on speaker please, Mom."

"Sure, honey."

"Can you hear me, Dad?"

"Yes, what's wrong?"

Hearing their voices provides me the kind of comfort that can only come from a parent and gives me strength I need.

"Paul's dead." Why did I blurt it out like that?

"What did you say, son?" Dad sounds confused.

I take a deep breath. "Paul killed himself."

"Oh, my God," Mom sounds on the brink of tears. "What happened?"

As I recount what has happened today, I leave out the gruesome parts for my mom's sake, knowing the investigative officer in Dad will want to know the details later.

"How are you holding up?" Dad asks.

"I'm, barely keeping it together." Then I lose it and surrender to my emotions. I hear Mom crying too.

"Paul was a damn good man, and I can't say how sorry I am to hear this news."

After mom and I pull ourselves together, Mom flips the switch to protective mode. "We're coming home."

"No, Mom, I don't want you to."

"We need to be there with you," she argues, while Dad remains silent.

"Really, I want you to enjoy your trip–Paul would want you to stay."

"We should be there with you, Lance."

"Mom, no, I'll be fine. I just needed to hear your voices. Please don't end your trip early."

"Nothing is more important than you, Lance."

"Dad, tell Mom I'll be fine. Jackson and the guys are here for me. Besides, trying to rearrange travel at the last minute will be a nightmare." This was all true, but mainly, I wouldn't be able to live with myself if they were not able to finish their dream vacation.

It took a lot of convincing, but eventually Mom gave in and agreed to stay in Italy as long as I promised to visit them once they returned home.

10

KELLIE

"Kellie! Get up, It's my wedding day." Gina screeches with excitement.

It feels as if I just closed my eyes a few minutes ago. It can't be that time yet and even if it is, how the hell is she so perky?

"Not yet. Please just five more minutes."

Between Gina's kicking and snoring, I barely slept. At one point I considered sleeping on the couch but was too tired to move.

If I'm honest with myself, it wasn't totally Gina's fault I couldn't sleep. Thoughts of Lance kept my mind occupied. I wondered what his likes and dislikes might be. Silly things I hoped to discover in time.

One question stuck in my mind. Could Lance date and maybe fall in love with a single parent and accept everything that comes along with raising a child that isn't his?

Fear of what his answer might be is the real reason I'm sleep deprived.

My plea for extra sleep is ignored by the bright-eyed bride-to-be who's now standing at the foot of the bed. I'm not ready to deal with her cheery disposition just yet. I have that sickly feeling in my stomach, the same one I get when I haven't slept enough.

"Come on, Kellie, get up." She doesn't seem to be suffering from a hangover.

"Ugh." I pull the covers over my head. "Just five, maybe ten more minutes, please."

"No way, Kellie, get up. The makeup and hair ladies are on their way to my mom's and we need to get moving now. We have a tight schedule."

With a loud groan I emerge from under the duvet and throw my pillow in her direction. She whips the covers off my body. "I hate you."

"You love me really, admit it." She laughs and directs me towards the bathroom.

"You're so bossy." I stomp away from her. "I feel sorry for Dirk."

It takes us an hour to finish packing Gina's honeymoon luggage and drive over to her mom's house.

On the ride over, Gina begins recalling bits and pieces from last night. Apparently, she was sober enough to remember Lance and hasn't stopped grilling me since pulling away from her place.

"Spill it, Kellie. Tell me all about Mr. Hottie from the bar last night." She asks with a cheeky grin.

"I can't believe you don't remember pushing dollar bills into the strippers g-string, but you remember seeing me with Lance."

Gina turns down the car radio she was singing along with earlier. "Quit deflecting. His name is Lance, that's a start. Keep going."

Wondering if she'll remember his last name, I give her a hint. "His full name is Lance Malloy." I pause, waiting for her response. She says nothing so I add the part I hope will make it click. "Deputy Lance Malloy." I keep my eyes on the road but can practically hear the cogs in her brain turning, trying to recall where she knows the name.

"Holy shit!" Her outburst makes me jump. "Your Deputy was in Heath's last night and you're just now telling me?" Gina is the only one who knows about my crush on Lance.

"Um, Gina. You were a little drunk at the time. In fact, I'm amazed at how alert you are this morning."

"Okay, you get a pass since I wasn't totally myself, but I want more details now."

"We didn't spend a lot of time together, so I don't have much to share. You already know he works for the Springhill Sheriff's Department."

"I can't believe it, Kellie. Who'd have thought you'd meet again."

"I know."

"Did he recognize and remember you?"

"After he introduced himself and I was certain he was the same man, I mentioned where I'd seen him before. I was shocked when he told me he remembered Rory and me from that day." Telling Gina has the butterflies in my stomach in a frenzy.

"That's great. It sounds like you made an impression on him too." Gina checks herself in the visor mirror and asks the big question. "Did you make plans to see each other again?"

"Funny you should ask. I decided to follow your advice and invited him to the wedding." I frown, wondering if I'd made the right decision.

"Holy fuck, Kellie." She's bouncing in her seat and clapping, unable to contain her excitement. "I'm so proud of you. I sort of remember saying something about inviting the man I saw holding your hand. I'm so glad you listened to me for a change. You two are totally meant to be."

"I can't believe I asked him to come especially since I won't be able to spend much time with him." Regret sneaks in with the realization this whole thing could blow up in my face.

Our conversation is cut short when we reach Gina's family home. Melanie is climbing out of her Jeep as I pull into the long driveway. From the scowl on her face, she doesn't look happy to be up and about this early either.

Gina unbuckles, turns in her seat, and gives my shoulder a reassuring squeeze. "There's no way in hell I will let you use my wedding to hide from Lance. Your duties don't take the whole day and I'll make sure you have time with him. Now hurry up."

Before I can argue about this being her special day, she jumps out of the car and runs into the house like an Olympic sprinter.

Melanie waits for me to grab my backpack from the trunk. "Damn, Kellie. You look terrible. What happened to you?"

"I didn't realize sharing a bed with Gina would leave me so sleep deprived." I chuckle before giving her the rundown of my night. "Have you ever slept in the same bed as Gina? She rolls from one side of the bed to the other. At one point she was turned around with her feet next to my head and kicked me in the face. I swear it was like an MMA fight, knee strikes, elbow jabs and a superpower submission hold. I have no idea how Dirk isn't bruised from head to toe."

Melanie wraps her arm around my shoulder. "You forget, I grew up with her. Gina's been kickboxing in her sleep since she was a kid. Come on, let's get one of Aunt Rachel's mimosas before the other girls show up."

"I'm going to stay out here and check on Rory before the craziness starts."

"Alright, I'll catch you inside."

I'm not sure why, but I have a strong need to hear Rory's voice before taking this leap of faith with Lance today.

Gina's mom has a quaint sitting area with a stone bench, surrounded by a circle of daisies. It looks to be the perfect spot to gather my thoughts and prepare for my time with Lance.

Unzipping my bag, I find my phone at the bottom and power it up. Seeing it only has ten percent battery left, I make a mental note to charge it when I get inside.

I've missed a text from Lance from early this morning.

Lance: Good morning beautiful. I hope I didn't wake you. Don't forget to send me the address to the venue. I'll be there as soon as my meeting with Paul is finished. I can't wait to see you again.

Shit, I was so tired last night, I forgot to text Lance the address for Gina's parents house where the wedding and reception will take place.

Me: Good morning Deputy. I'm excited to see you too! Both the wedding and reception are at Gina's parent's house. 15 Greenville Drive, Springhill. See you later. Kellie x

Not expecting a reply from Lance, I switch over to *FaceTime* and speak to Rory and Mom.

I can hear my mom before I see her. "Say hello to Addy K, Rory."

I wonder if Rory has the phone in her hands as the images are bouncing around. A feeling of contentment and happiness runs through me. This is the boost I needed to help me get through the day.

"Sit down, Rory and talk to Aunt Kellie"

"Rory, can you hear me?" I hear her giggles. "You're going to make me dizzy moving the phone around like that."

Finally, the picture on the screen is still and I get a perfect view of my parent's kitchen ceiling.

"Addy K, where are you?" The image on the screen switches from the ceiling to a close-up of Rory's nose.

"Hang on, Kellie." Mom has endless patience with her granddaughter. "Rory, you can't hold it that close to your face. Let me help you."

A little more shifting and I see my mom sitting with Rory in her lap. My rambunctious niece has a serious case of bedhead. Mom looks happy but worn out too. I know the feeling.

"Good Morning. Did you two just wake up?"

"Hi, Addy K." Rory grabs a piece of Gram Grams toast and licks the strawberry jam coating it. As they say, like mother like daughter. Leslie loved strawberry jam too.

"Oh, no. You know this little one was up with the roosters. She already tired out Grumpa after an early morning tea party for Mr. Deputy Bear and her other stuffed animal friends."

"So, I'm assuming Dad's napping already." I picture him snoring in his recliner, still holding the TV remote as per usual. "Mom. Don't just let her lick the jam. I don't let her do that at home."

"It's not going to hurt her, Kellie. She'll have fresh veggies from our garden at lunch but while at Grandma's I make the rules, remember." I am politely dismissed from having an opinion on her eating habits while at my parent's house.

"Fine." I've learned to pick and choose my battles with both Rory and my parents. This is one battle I'm not going to wage today. "Rory, that's so cool. You get to pick veggies with Gram Gram. Are you excited?"

Placing the soggy toast on the plate in front of her, Rory looks up and I see the mess she's made on her face. A red dot of jam sits on the tip of her nose.

"Yep. I pull carrots from dirt." Before I can tell Rory to

wash her face, she shoots me a cheesy grin. It's the same mischievous smile I remember her momma shining back at me over the breakfast table. It makes me miss my sister each time she does it, yet it brings me happiness getting these surprise glimpses of Leslie.

Refusing to let my thoughts drift into the past, I focus on Rory and the wedding.

"Okay, you two. I have to go. Have fun gardening. Save me some sugar peas and carrots and we can make a chicken pot pie with them tomorrow."

"Yay! Pot pie." Rory loves playing in the flour and using the cookie cutters for the crust.

Gina leans out the second-floor window and yells. "Hurry up, Kellie."

"I need to go. Gina's yelling for me to get upstairs. I love you both and tell dad I love him too."

"We love you too. I'll drop Rory off tomorrow afternoon so you can sleep in."

"Thanks, Mom. Bye, Rory. Be good, I love you."

"Love you lots, Addy K."

With images of Rory's smile running through my mind, I jog up the stairs and prepare for the big day. Not just Gina's, but my day with Lance, too.

The outdoor wedding ceremony was everything Gina dreamed it would be. The sky was the perfect shade of baby blue with billowy white clouds. A slight breeze blew through the surrounding trees, helping cool the guests as they watched Dirk and Gina celebrate the happiest day of their lives.

While standing up with Gina at the gazebo, I searched for Lance, but couldn't find him in the large crowd. Not knowing anybody. I imagined he had sat at the back.

After standing for what felt like a million pictures, the bridesmaids and groomsmen were dismissed while Gina and Dirk continued posing in front of the setting sun.

Server's wander amongst the wedding guests with trays of hors d'oeuvres and flutes of champagne while Gina and Dirk finish with the photographer. Accepting a crystal glass from Dirk's best man, Stephan, I excuse myself in search of Lance. Finding him in this crowd of over one hundred guests won't be easy.

Sipping my champagne, I walk the perimeter of the crowd, to a table with the seating chart. Since Lance was added at the last minute, I have no idea where he will sit during dinner.

My heart sinks when I see his name on one of the few remaining tent cards still sitting on the table. Hopefully, he just hasn't picked it up yet and we are both wandering in search of the other.

Needing my phone, I walk into Gina's old bedroom. Unplugging it from the charger I left it on earlier, I decide to send a text to find out where my plus-one is.

Me: *Hi Lance. Were you able to find the house okay? I can't find you in this crowd of guests. Text me back and we can find a spot to meet. Kellie x*

While waiting for a reply, I sit on the window bench and watch as the guests take their seats for dinner service. I'm deliriously happy for my friends, but a pang of jealousy pulls at my heart. Will I ever have a day like this?

Knowing someone will come looking for me soon, I send one more text before returning to the reception.

Me: *Lance. I'm sorry to bother you, but I'm worried. Are* *you okay? Please text me when you can talk. I'm here if you need me. Kellie x*

I continue to stare at the phone, praying for a quick reply but ten minutes later, I'm left hanging. I make my way back to the party.

Dinner is being served and I'll be missed if I'm not there to give the maid of honor speech. Without pockets, I tuck my phone into the side of my bra under my dress.

Gina finds me as I make my way to the head table.

"Where's Lance?"

"Don't worry about him. You've got better things to think about right now. Dinner is just the beginning. I have a long to do list for you; your first dance, tossing the bouquet and cutting the cake."

She doesn't need to know about the unsubstantiated worry and fear I feel. My mood shouldn't ruin her day.

While dinner was being served, I scouted about with my eyes, hoping Trish was on her best behavior. I can't find her, and thinking about it, I only remember seeing her before the ceremony. Either way, she hasn't made a scene and for that I'm grateful.

As the dinner dishes were being cleared, the DJ turned down the volume of the soft mood music. "Could you all stand and welcome the bride and groom to the center of the dance floor." We all stood and cheered the happy couple.

"If everyone would raise their glasses and toast Mr. and Mrs. Thompson."

Amongst the rapturous cheers, Dirk and Gina reach the center of the parquet floor and kiss sweetly, before walking away from the other to stand in opposite corners.

The room falls silent as the DJ introduces their first dance as husband and wife.

I anxiously wait to hear what song Gina and Dirk chose

for their first dance. The opening bars of *Ed Sheeran's Thinking Out Loud* flows from the speakers. I'm stunned with the choreographed moves my friends are performing. They have obviously put a lot of effort into making this moment special for everybody there. I suspect private dance lessons are responsible because Dirk usually has two left feet and right now, the two glide across the floor like Hollywood film stars of old. I feel a lump in my throat. The love between them is palpable. It's like nobody else is in the room but them.

It's my turn to dance with the best man, Stephan. The other bridesmaids and groomsmen partnered up as we danced to *Brad Paisley's She's Everything*. This was my moment in the spotlight and one I wasn't looking forward to. I smile and sway to the music, barely touching Stephan before we switch partners with Dirk and Gina.

Dirk pulls me into a brotherly hug. "You look beautiful, Kellie. Thank you for being a part of our special day."

"I'm so happy for you and Gina." I hug him tight before the music takes us and he spins me round the floor. I am taken aback by his nifty moves. This confirms the dance lesson theory.

Then, he kisses my cheek and spins me back into Stephan's arms, possessively taking hold of his bride once more. I guess Gina won't be dancing with anyone but her husband tonight.

Dirk had to let Gina go one more time for the father-daughter dance which included a mother and son dance at the same time.

I feel emotional and lost to the dance. The fantasy of dancing with my father at my own wedding fills my thoughts. I picture Rory standing on Grumpa's feet while we dance to *Tim McGraws' My Little Girl*. I quickly glance around to check if anyone is watching before I wipe away my tears.

Dancing over with, it's time to party. The DJ cranks up the

volume. The girls kick their heels into the corner as *Kool & The Gang's Celebration* packs out the dance floor.

Gina is dancing in a tight circle of family and friends while singing *We Are Family* by *Sister Sledge*. Her smile says it all. This is the wedding day she's always dreamed of.

"Kellie!" Gina hobbles over to me lifting her layers of satin and tulle. She looks like a penguin waddling my way. "You need to dance with me. Come on." Gina drags me into the middle of the group as *Girls Just Want to Have Fun* by *Cyndi Lauper* blasts through the speakers. For the rest of the night, I danced and left all my worries behind while I celebrated my best friend's wedding.

When it came time for the bouquet toss, I purposely stood off to the side and smiled for the pictures. Little did I know there was a conspiracy afoot.

The DJ spoke to the guests. "Alright ladies, step onto the dance floor and let's see who the next bride will be. On the count of three." There is a collective hush around the room. "One. Two. Three." On three, all the ladies who were crowded around, stepped away and the flowers landed right in my hands. I stood, horrified, not knowing what to do while Gina laughed her ass off. I had to admire her because this little trick of hers had been skillfully kept from me. I'd like to say I was angry, but inside, my heart beat fast while I wished for the same happiness Gina felt.

After waving goodbye to Dirk and Gina, I gather my things and drive the short distance to my unusually quiet house.

Parking in my driveway, I turn off my car ignition and check my phone one more time, hoping for a message from Lance. Still nothing.

· · ·

Me: Hi Lance. I'm home from the wedding now. I hope you're okay. I'm really worried. Please text me when you can. Kellie x

Pressing send, I stare at the screen, willing it to show me Lance is typing a reply.

I haven't prayed since Leslie died but something inside me says it's time to check in with God again.

Please God, protect Lance and all those around him. Bring them home safe today and always.

A cold gust of wind shakes my car as I finish my prayer.

With my hands full of bags, I let them fall to the floor in the entry way. I'm too tired to care about the mess and with Rory still at my parents I don't have to worry about picking it up right now. Exhaustion is winning the war over a tidy house tonight.

Every muscle in my body aches and is screaming at me to soak for hours in a bubble bath. Having a quiet house for once, I plan on doing just that.

Switching on the floor lamp, I grab the long strap of my oversized purse and drag it behind me into the kitchen.

An audible grumble from my stomach reminds me I didn't eat much today. Between worrying about Lance and other wedding party duties, I was too busy to care. Staying busy was a welcome distraction, keeping my thoughts away from what could possibly be wrong with Lance.

When I finally decided to grab a bite to eat, I was pulled away for more pictures, Dirk and Gina's first dance, the bouquet toss, you name it. Twice the waiters took away my plate before I had more than a bite or two.

Too tired to cook a hot meal, I open the cupboard, grab a large bowl and a spoon from the dishwasher. Checking inside the pantry, I realize my choices are slim. Dry cereal or nothing. The one with raisins was on sale, but it tastes terrible. I choose the box of Loop cereal, as Rory calls it, along with the carton of milk from the fridge.

The sweet smell from the sugary cereal drifts up as I pour it into the bowl. I pop a few loops into my mouth before pouring the last of the milk over the top. I guess I'll be shopping for groceries before Rory comes home tomorrow.

After the cereal has been eaten, I pick up the bowl and drink the leftover milk. Why anyone would throw out the cereal milk is beyond me. It's the best part. I place the empty bowl and spoon into the sink, take my purse off the counter and walk down the hall to my bedroom.

Sitting on the edge of my mattress, I flop back and close my eyes.

I didn't realize I'd fallen asleep until the buzz from an incoming text startles me awake. Searching for my phone, I hear the faint vibrations coming from the bottomless pit of my purse. Impatience at trying to dig through the junk in my bag has me turning the contents onto my bed.

Unlocking the screen with my thumb, I read the message from Lance.

Lance: Kellie. I'm sorry I missed the wedding. We had an emergency today. I'm okay, sort of. I know it's late, but I could use a friend right now. But I'd like to see you if you're around? **Lance x**

Texting back and forth won't do. I dial Lance's number and thankfully he answers immediately.

"Kellie." Lance's voice is hoarse.

"Lance, what's wrong. Where are you?" My concern has me pacing around my bedroom.

"I'm at my house. I can't explain over the phone. Can I come see you?"

"That's fine. I'll send you my address." I suppose I should be more cautious having a man I barely know over to my house, but in my heart, I know I'm safe with Lance.

"I'll be there soon. And Kellie, thanks..." His voice breaks and I hear a soft sniffle as if he's been crying.

"Are you sure you're okay to drive? I can come get you if you want."

"Nah, I'll have Jackson drop me off. I'll be there soon. Thanks for letting me come see you."

"Of course. I'll see you soon."

Lance's usual strong, confident voice was replaced with a softer tone I hadn't heard before. So low, I barely caught the tremor in his last words.

Be patient, I tell myself. I don't know what has happened yet to cause him such distress.

Get yourself cleaned up and worry when there is something to worry about.

11

LANCE

After the tough conversation with my parents about Paul, I laid back on my bed for what I thought would be a short nap, but it turned into hours. The sun was out when I closed my eyes and now my bedroom is dark with only the moonlight streaming in through my open curtains.

I'm not sure what prompted me to text Kellie this late, but I'm glad I did. The thought of seeing her brings on an unexplainable wave of comfort.

Standing under the scalding hot shower, I scrub my body furiously with a sponge, but it does nothing to wash away the stain of Paul's blood I felt still coated the skin on my hands.

What went wrong? What could I have done differently to stop Paul from pulling the trigger?

Running through possible scenarios in my mind is when I would normally call my partner. Using teamwork to brainstorm and work out a case. I never imagined there would be a time when Paul wouldn't be around for me to bounce ideas off.

I'm still in shock, not ready to accept I'll never see him again. The rational part of my brain tells me reality is about to hit me hard. It's a question of when not if.

For now, it's just a constant weight pushing down on my chest. Maybe this was how Paul felt after Jane died. I choke back more tears knowing that if I let them come again, I'll struggle to get them under control long enough to ask Jackson to drive me to Kellie's.

"Fuck you, Paul! Fuck you for leaving me!" Anger bubbles inside. An emotion I don't want to feel, but it's there, gnawing away at me. I lean my head against the tile and yell out my heartbreak.

Jackson knocks on the bathroom door. "Hey, Lance, I'm glad you're awake. I made some sandwiches if you're hungry." It's his subtle way of checking on me.

"Thanks," I call out. "Give me just another few minutes."

Turning off the hot water, I stand in the shower, trembling, as images of Paul flash like a slide show through my mind.

The day we met is suddenly crystal clear. Standing in line to pick up our recruit bags. Each of us covered in mud after attacking the obstacle course. Sitting on the riverbank fishing and never catching a damn thing. Paul on one knee asking Jane to be his wife.

The next images popping into my mind almost causes me to collapse against the wall. Paul's bloody and lifeless body on the floor. The gurney being pushed into the ambulance. The last goodbye to my best friend in that tiny hospital room that has seen so much death over the years.

Each memory circles me like a cyclone. Horrific images of finding my partner mingle with happier times. Just like a destructive twister, memories don't discriminate, grabbing everyone in its path, tossing them in the air, before slamming them back to earth a shattered mess.

That's exactly how I feel. Shattered and useless.

Walking out of my room the smell of the grilled sandwich turns my stomach. I have no appetite, but I know if I don't eat something Jackson won't let up.

Jackson has set a plate and bottle of water for me on the

dining room table. I'm certain I'm dehydrated and my muscles throb as if I've run a marathon. Twisting the cap off the water I down the entire bottle before taking my seat.

"How are you feeling?" Jackson's attempt at small talk sucks.

"How do you think I feel? I feel like my best friend just killed himself." I take a bite of the sandwich I can't taste. "Sorry, I'm being an ass. Thanks for the food."

Jackson sits across from me and picks at his own sandwich. "My fault for asking a stupid question. Is there anything I can do?"

Taking another bite, I chew slowly while carefully picking my words.

"Actually, yeah, there is something I need to ask you." After all he's done for me today, I'm hopeful my request won't offend him. "I don't want to be around our work family right now."

"Lance, I already told you I'm not leaving you alone tonight."

"I know and I'm glad you're here, but I can't stay cooped up in this house either. I've already had to turn my phone off with all the calls and messages pouring in. I don't want anyone coming over unannounced either."

"So, what do you have in mind."

"I was thinking about driving over to Kellie's place."

"Is Kellie the woman you were talking to last night?"

"Yes. You probably think I'm an idiot, but it feels right. Instead of fighting my instinct, I want to go with it and see her."

"Lance, I'm not judging you. I saw the look on your face this morning when you were talking about her. How does this sound? I'm not keen on you driving so I'll take you over and stay or leave, your choice. If I leave, you can call me to pick you up, but you have to promise me you won't be on your own tonight. Got it?"

"I was hoping you'd understand. Let me finish this sandwich you made and I'll be ready."

"Well, it could have been a five-star meal if you learned how to stock your refrigerator. By the way, there was a science experiment growing in a red bowl on the bottom shelf. I figured I'd toss it out for you." Jackson's lighthearted joke changes the mood if only for a moment, but I'll take anything I can get right now.

Taking the last bite, I carry our empty plates to the kitchen and place both in the dishwasher.

"Kellie sent me her address earlier. I'm ready when you are."

Kellie's house isn't too far from mine. She lives on a cul-de-sac on the opposite end of our small town.

In front of Kellie's house, chalk drawings on the asphalt are illuminated by the bright streetlights. A large smiling bear, a big blue house and two stick figures holding hands, one shorter than the other. I imagine these are Rory's drawings, probably with a little help from her aunt.

Turning to thank Jackson for the ride, I see he's already unbuckled his seat belt. "What? Did you think I was just going to pull up and push you out the door?"

"I don't need a babysitter, Jackson." His hovering is beginning to annoy me.

"I know you don't but you're about to unload a lot on this woman and even if you don't need me there, maybe she could use a little support."

Blowing out a sigh, I give in. "For the hundredth time tonight, you're right. Let's go."

As we walk up to the house, the motion sensor lights turn on. I'm glad she has that security feature in place.

I knock twice on the door and step back as doubt creeps

into my mind. *What made me think this was a good idea?* Before I can get too far into my head, I hear the deadbolt turn. It's too late to walk away now.

Kellie opens the door with a smile and stands partially hidden behind it. Her dark shoulder length hair is damp, and I don't see a hint of makeup on her flawless skin. She doesn't need it. An oversized T-shirt proudly announces she is the world's best auntie, with two tiny blue handprints I assume are Rory's.

As she opens the door fully, I notice she's wearing black yoga pants and her feet are bare. When I look up to her face to greet her, her smile is gone and replaced with what looks like concern.

"Hi, Kellie…" She has no idea why I'm on her porch, yet she's here with me. I want to say something to bring back her smile. Tell her how beautiful she is, that being here has eased some of my heartache. Only it hurts too much to speak.

Without warning, Kellie wraps her arms around my waist, laying her cheek over my heart. This is the woman I watched comfort Rory all those months ago and now she's taking care of me. I return the embrace and inhale the sweet honey fragrance of her shampoo.

Jackson clears his throat. "Hi, Kellie. I'm Deputy Jackson Locke, I work with Lance. May we come in?"

"Oh, my gosh. I'm so sorry. Yes, please come in."

Kellie steps aside. I look about the cozy house. Signs of Rory are everywhere. Not in an untidy way. In the corner is a child's table with a tea set. Near the window is an art easel with a finger-painted masterpiece pinned to it. A stark contrast to the apartment she lived in with her mother. This is the home Rory deserves to grow up in.

"It's nice to meet you, Jackson. Why don't you two sit in here and I'll get us something to drink?"

I sit opposite Jackson on the leather couch and continue looking around the room.

Beside an overstuffed chair, is a wicker basket filled with books. I bet Kellie and Rory cuddle up and read together before bedtime in this spot. I notice a stack of children's movies on the bookshelf over on the far wall.

In front of the couch is a glass table. A children's version of treasure island and another of King Arthur and the Knights of the Round table catch my eye. My dad used to read those to me.

"It's nice to meet you too, Kellie. You don't have to go to any trouble."

"It's no trouble at all. Is coffee okay or would you like something else?"

Since I can't seem to find my voice, Jackson answers. "Coffee would be great, thanks."

"I'll be right back. Please make yourself at home."

Kellie is barely two steps away from us when Jackson whispers his concerns. "Lance, are you sure about this? You barely know this girl."

"Yes...No...I don't know." I scrub my hand over my face. "For some reason this is where my heart says I need to be. Today has been the worst day of my life and all I want is to feel some sense of normality and I think Kellie is the one that can help me with that."

"Lance, nothing is going to make what happened today disappear, but if being with your girl will help make tonight bearable, then I support you just as I always do."

"Jackson, Kellie is not my girl." Standing just steps away, judging by the stunned look on her face, I suspect she's heard our entire conversation.

"Are you sure about that, Lance?"

If Kellie heard us, she's doing a great job pretending she didn't. "Um, I'm sorry, I'm out of milk, but I have some powdered cream if you need it."

Jackson stands and takes the tray from Kellie.

"Thanks. Let me move Rory's books and toys then you can set the tray on the table."

"Shoot, I'm sorry, Kellie, I didn't even think about how late it is and us waking up Rory. We shouldn't have called. Come on, Jackson we better leave." It's more than waking Rory that has me wanting to escape. Incredible fear I have about reliving today has surfaced and facing it right now has my heart pounding. I can feel the sweat beading on my upper lip and my breathing erratic.

Sitting beside me, Kellie gently places her hand on my thigh, sending an unexpected wave of calm washing over me. "It's okay, Lance. Rory is with my parents for the night. I'm a little confused why you're both here, but you said you needed a friend and I want to be here for you. Please tell me what's wrong?"

My stomach rolls and heart races at the thought of saying the words out loud.

Finally, Jackson breaks the silence.

"You already know there was an emergency today from the text Lance said he sent you. Well it goes much deeper than that. We lost one of our own today." He pauses when Kellie gasps.

"Lance's partner, Paul, took his own life this morning which is why Lance missed the wedding. Although we are all grieving, Lance is struggling the most. He asked me to bring him here and since I don't want him to be alone, I agreed to drive him."

"Oh, Lance. I'm so sorry." She clasps my hands in hers.

Listening to Jackson tell Kellie that brief run down of my day feels odd. By leaving out the details, Jackson has left it to me to fill in the blanks. But first I need to explain why it's important for me to be here with her.

"My head and my heart led me to you. It feels like having you by my side will help me get through the worst night of my life." I keep my eyes cast toward the floor, afraid of her reaction to how vulnerable I am in this moment. "I need to talk or maybe just sit in silence." I look up and see the only woman I want to be with right now. "Don't ask me why, but I think being with you will make things seem better."

"Lance..." Kellie gently places her fingertips under my chin, tilting my head upward, allowing her to see my tear-filled eyes. "I'm glad you called me and that I can be here for you."

"It may seem stupid, but I need a friend who isn't a cop. Someone I can talk to who isn't going to analyze the situation and give me their expert opinion on how and why Paul killed himself. I know it's selfish to unload all of this on you, but I was hoping that tonight, that friend could be you."

Jackson pushes himself up from the couch. "It looks like you have it under control here. Rather than me sticking around, I think you two could use some time together." Reaching into his wallet, he hands Kellie his business card. "Kellie, if you need anything, not just tonight, anytime, please call me."

"Lance, if you need me to come back, I am just a phone call away." He pulls me into a hug and slaps my back.

Kellie walks Jackson to the door but I can't hear their conversation. She gives him a hug then closes the door behind him.

Returning to the couch, she angles her body towards me. Nervous tension hangs in the air.

"Would you like me to pour you some coffee or maybe fix you something to eat?"

"Nothing for me, really. I ate earlier, and only did it to appease Jackson, but my stomach is in knots." It's then I realize I've wrapped my arms around my body as if to keep the pain and hurt inside.

"I won't ask if you're okay because I know you're not. How could you be? If you want to talk about today, I'll listen.

If you just want to sit in silence, we can do that too. Whatever you need, I'm here for you."

Kellie's words cover me like a warm blanket. She doesn't push me to talk, but it gives me the courage to open up and tell her what happened. "I was supposed to meet Paul this morning, to talk him into accepting some sort of professional help." I take a deep breath. "He was never the same after his wife died, and this time of year was always the hardest on him." Kellie sits quietly, allowing me to share my story at a pace I'm comfortable with. "Jackson and I had a plan. We met at Paul's house, but we were too late. Paul killed himself sometime after leaving Heath's last night."

"Oh, God, my heart is breaking for you." Tears fill her eyes. She didn't know Paul, but she cares about people.

I realize I'm speaking as if I'm writing a report. Not a lot of emotion behind my words, just facts. The emotional wound has been open all day now and I just don't have anything else to let out. "There was nothing the doctors could do; he was already gone."

"I'm so sorry, Lance. I wish there was some way I could take away the pain you're feeling."

"Saying goodbye to him was the hardest thing I've ever had to do."

Kellie climbs onto my lap, wrapping her arms around my neck and cries her own tears. Using my thumb, I brush them away.

"Kellie, you have such a kind heart. I saw it the day you protected and saved Rory and now you're protecting me."

"We all need help sometimes, Lance. You can't always be the hero." Kellie snuggles into my chest.

"It's getting late. Maybe I should call for a ride and let you get some sleep."

When I try to move her off my lap onto the couch, she holds firm. "No way, mister. I promised Jackson I wouldn't let you out of my sight, so you're stuck with me."

"Okay, but I don't have the energy to think or talk about today anymore."

"Then we don't have to talk. How about a movie? We can watch something on Netflix or maybe a goofy Disney movie from Rory's collection. Those always change my mood and usually help me drift off to sleep." Her cute giggle has me cracking a smile.

"Do you have popcorn?"

"Yep, and it's the real kind too. I can pop it over the stove and pour melted butter all over it. You pick something for us to watch and I'll make the popcorn." She moves to climb off my lap but stops and looks deep into my eyes. She sees the real me. The parts I keep hidden. Despite my sorrow, I'm enchanted by her. She's some kind of special.

When she bites her lip, I'm reminded of the sweet kiss we shared. I desperately want more but guilt stabs at me. My friend lies dead in a morgue and I'm wanting to make out with a girl I hardly know. What the fuck is wrong with me?

But then, I remember Paul's words from last night. If I really believe Kellie is the one I'm meant to love, I need to hold on tight and not let go. I brush a strand of Kellie's hair behind her ear and lean in slowly. Perhaps she will reject my advances, perhaps she won't, but I feel compelled to try.

When she leans in and our lips meet, I freeze, guilt getting the best of me. Sometimes being the good guy really sucks.

I want to lose myself in this woman and forget everything that has happened today but that's not fair to Kellie.

"Um, Kellie."

"I don't know what came over me. I'm so sorry. Your friend just died and here I am climbing all over you. I'm so embarrassed." Her cheeks flush and she won't look at me.

"Please don't be embarrassed. I want you..." I run my hand through my hair in frustration. "Boy do I want you. But I want us to happen at the right time. Not because I'm trying to cover up the hurt inside that's eating me up." Kellie slides off my lap and sits beside me.

"I understand." She blows out a breath and rushes to her feet.

"The chemistry between us is stronger than anything I've ever felt before. But maybe we should wait a little longer until I can get my head straight."

"Okay, let's go back to plan A. You're picking the movie and I'm making popcorn." She quickly dashes off into the kitchen.

I sit back and close my eyes. Part of me knows Paul is smiling down right now telling me to not fuck this up.

A few minutes later, Kellie returns with a huge bowl of greasy, buttery popcorn and cues up the first thing Netflix suggests. The sound is low and neither of us are paying much attention to the movie. It wasn't long before Kellie places a pillow on my lap and stretches her legs out on the cushions. A pink, fuzzy blanket rests on the arm of the couch. I pull it over her just as her eyes close. Craving silence, I aim the remote control toward the TV and sit in the dark, replaying today's events over and over until sleep finally takes me.

12

KELLIE

I had not intended on falling asleep on the couch but waking up in Lance's arms feels like a dream. After hearing a small portion of what he experienced yesterday, I felt crushed, and I didn't even know Paul. God knows how wounded Lance feels losing his best friend because he has only begun to scratch the surface of his grief.

As he begins to absorb the shock and comes to terms with losing his friend, he will need a lot of support. I know because I've been there when dealing with Leslie's death.

When he's ready to talk, I'll listen. The time will come for him to vent his rage and fury, but I'll try my best to remember it's just part of the process and nothing personal toward me.

I spewed angry words on my family while working through my grief. My actions were inexcusable, but for family and friends who love me, they understood the root of my frustration. No judgements were made, or grudges held.

Now, Lance deserves the same understanding.

He's sleeping so I'll revel in this peaceful moment, snuggled against him. Goosebumps cover my body when I think about last night's kiss. It could have led to much more, but I understand Lance's hesitation and agree waiting is the better option. Especially now. Our time will come. There is no reason to rush or complicate what we have.

We've only shared a few light kisses, but my heart is all in.

Lance has a strong, almost protective hold around my waist, but I manage to wiggle my way out of his grasp and tip toe into the bathroom. A quick shower to tame my unruly hair, brush my teeth and put on some fresh clothes and I'm ready to face the day.

I sneak a peek at the sleeping giant on my living room couch. His floppy hair covers his face. I wonder how comfortable he could really be with his long body stretched out and his feet hanging over the edge.

Waking up a few times during the night I watched Lance as he slept. It was the most relaxed I'd seen him since he arrived. I was aware his space on the couch was limited so tried to fit in around him, but each time I moved he would stir so I decided to stay put.

Time for breakfast. I know Lance barely ate yesterday and wonder if he is open to a hearty meal. A man his size must eat a lot.

Looking through the refrigerator, I take out eggs, bacon, and grab the pancake mix from the pantry.

A few minutes later, while standing in front of the stove, I feel strong arms slide around my waist.

"Good Morning. How did you sleep?" Lance kisses my cheek and reaches around me to steal a slice of bacon from the plate on the back burner.

"That little couch of yours is a bit too short for me, but having you near, made all the difference." He chews quickly. "Mmmm." The noise tells me he enjoyed the stolen piece of bacon. It seems his appetite has returned.

"There are plenty of pancakes, eggs and bacon, unless you eat it all right now." I playfully swat his hand away before he takes more bacon. His chuckle is music to my ears.

"It sure smells delicious in here."

127

"There's a lot. I hope you're hungry." As I turn to place the stack of pancakes on the table, Lance takes the plate from my hands and spins me into his arms.

"I think it's you that smells so appetizing. Sweet, like honey and something else I can't quiet place."

"It's probably my shampoo." I giggle when Lance nuzzles and tickles my neck with his early morning beard.

Lance's playfulness and flirting almost makes me forget why he came to my house last night.

I get the feeling he is trying to push his emotions about Paul's death to the side, only delaying the inevitable. His positivity would be easy for me to go along with, but I can't let him bottle up his feelings. I'm not a professional in dealing with grief and losing a loved one, but I know this behavior won't help in the long run.

I still check in with my counselor when things overwhelm me, and it's been over six months since I lost Leslie. I'm certain the Sheriff's department will offer grief counseling but finding a way to broach the subject will be the tricky part.

"Sit down and eat while the food is still hot." I'm aware I sound like a nagging wife. "Do you want coffee or juice?"

"You don't have to wait on me, Kellie."

"I know, but you're my guest." I hold up the coffee carafe and bottle of juice for him to choose.

"So, which one?"

"Black coffee is fine."

Placing the mug in front of Lance, I notice his food hasn't been touched. Perhaps he was waiting for me to start eating.

"Rory says I make the best pancakes in the world. Dig in and let me know what you think?" I take a bite of my own breakfast and watch Lance carefully.

He pours syrup over the pancake, cuts in into several small pieces, and moves it around the plate a few times before trying it. Lance gives no indication if he likes the food or not. He swallows hard.

"So, how is it?"

"I'm sorry, Kellie. I thought I was hungry." He pushes the plate away. "I think that bacon earlier has upset my stomach. Can you excuse me a moment?" He pushes himself away from the table and rushes down the hall.

Concerned, I follow him and lightly knock on the bathroom door. "Hey, Lance, are you okay? Can I get you anything?"

"I'll be okay. It was just an upset stomach. I'll be out in just a bit." I feel instant relief at hearing his voice.

"There's a new toothbrush and things in the bottom left drawer. You're welcome to use what you need."

"Thanks, Kellie."

Knowing I can't manage this situation alone, I find Jackson's card and dial his number.

"Deputy Locke speaking." Jackson answers in a professional voice.

"Hi Jackson. It's Kellie."

"Good Morning. What can I do for you?"

"It's not an emergency so don't panic, but I'm afraid Lance isn't doing well this morning."

"Okay, I'll come over now. Tell me exactly what's going on." I hear the jangle of keys from his end then a door close.

"Everything seemed fine this morning until we sat down to have breakfast.

"Okay."

"He excused himself to go to the bathroom, saying he's not feeling well. I was worried and checked on him." I hear my bathroom door open. "He's coming back."

"Alright, keep him there. I won't be long."

"Hey, Kellie. I think I should get going. Maybe it's a stomach flu. I wouldn't want to get you sick."

Lance doesn't look at me while speaking. I assume it's because he's lying to me, and himself.

"I called Jackson."

Now I had his attention. "Why?" he snapped.

"Because I thought you might want to leave if you were sick."

"I'm a grown man, Kellie."

"I know that, but I thought if you needed to freshen up, Jackson could make sure you got home okay."

"Is he on his way now?"

"Yeah." I'd only told him half the truth. A little white lie was told for the right reasons but he was pissed at me. A knock on the front door saves me from fumbling through more lies. "Perfect timing. That's probably Jackson now."

Scooting around Lance, I answer the door without checking the peep hole. At this hour, who else would it be.

I try to sound upbeat and steady. "Hi, Jackson. Please come in."

"Good morning, Kellie." He looks to the broken man standing behind me. "Hey, Lance. I thought you might need a ride this morning. How 'bout I give you a minute with your girl. I'll meet you in the truck." Jackson makes eye contact with me. He's grateful I called him, that much is evident without words. He doesn't wait for an answer and leaves, closing the door behind him.

"So, what's all this talk about me being your girl? That's twice now. Once last night, and now Jackson just said it."

"Well, I know things seem to be moving fast, but I'd like to think you're my girl."

"Really?" I don't know how to respond.

"I'd like that, you know, for us to be exclusive."

"Well…" I'm lost for words.

"How does that sound to you?"

His hopeful tone brings a smile to my face. I finally find my voice. "Lance, I've been yours for longer than you know and have no desire to date anyone but you."

Seeing his wide grin and bright eyes warms my heart. He wraps his arms around my waist. "The universe works in mysterious ways, Kellie." He plants a kiss on my forehead. "I think you were meant to come into my life and help lead me through the darkness."

He lifts my chin gently and his lips brush mine. His sweet kiss leaves me weak at the knees, but I want more than sweet this time. I want his kiss to tell me I'm his girl and he's my man. I want him to see me as the light in his life, the one constant that will always pull him back to steady ground.

His kiss is slow and tender, not what I want. Impatience creeps in. Without invitation, I pull him in for a long, lingering kiss. There is passion but forcefulness that takes me by surprise. I want him to see me for the woman I am, loving, strong, powerful, capable, protective, all those things that will help heal his heart. Finally, Lance takes the hint and tips my head slightly. Together, we find our rhythm, each satisfying the hunger inside. It isn't our first kiss, but it's the way it should be.

Lance pulls away, our foreheads touch and we are syncopated as one. We take long, deep breaths. "I have to go." He brushes his nose over mine. I giggle like a schoolgirl in the first flushes of love.

"I know, but it's hard to let you go." It's not like me to show my vulnerable side, but for him, anything is possible. "Promise you'll come back to me?" The lump in my throat keeps me from voicing my fear—that I won't see or hear from Lance again.

He kisses me quickly and opens the door. "I'll call you later tonight, promise."

The door closes and I crumble to the floor in a heap as memories of Leslie's death and the aftermath infiltrate my thoughts.

Those first days when I wished I'd died right along with my sister. The incredible pain that surged through every nerve in my body, keeping me in bed for days. I wanted it to go away with the swish of a magic wand. Instead it took a village of family, friends, and professionals to pull me out of my depression.

I found my way through as Lance will, given time. He is going through hell, and I desperately want to help him. I just found Lance and can't lose him now.

13

LANCE

Walking away from Kellie is harder than I thought it would be. The figurative blanket of comfort she provided was everything I needed last night, but today, it's not nearly enough.

Each step I take away from her house felt like a weighted sled dragging behind me.

I heard her rise then take a shower. I wanted to join her, but my body wouldn't move. Not because of sleeping on that tiny couch, but because my head was jampacked with images from yesterday. I felt anxious, breathless, out of control. I forced the smile onto my face, even stealing a slice of bacon, wanting a touch of normality. But I was in a living hell, unable to maintain any façade. I struggled to catch my breath long enough to try and pretend I felt better.

The smallest things catapulted me back to Paul's house, to the hospital room where I said my goodbye. Even Kellie offering me a cup of coffee forced me to revisit handing Jackson the paper cup before knocking on Paul's door. That simple, kind gesture triggering an anxiety attack was unexpected.

Initially seething when Kellie told me she'd called Jackson, deep down I was grateful and relieved because she took the first step I was hesitant to make. If she hadn't made the call, I might have kept up the pretense all was fine, just like Paul did.

Taking deep breaths, I filled my lungs with fresh air, the feeling of pressure easing somewhat.

"You ready?" Jackson asked.

"Yeah!" Slamming Jacksons truck door, I keep my eye's forward and buckle up. I'm not up to talking but I doubt Jackson will be swayed by my refusal to unburden myself.

"Thanks for the ride, but I'm not in the mood to talk right now."

"Lance, I'll give you time to get your head together, but I'm not leaving you alone." Jackson slides his aviators on. "Now make your choice; your house or mine."

"I want to go home please, but can you keep people away. I'm not ready to listen to everyone's sympathy right now." I lean my head against the side window and close my eyes wanting to clear my cluttered mind. "I know I need help, and I'm not pushing you away Jackson, but I need it at my pace."

"Yeah, man. I can do that for you, but I have some requirements too. It's nothing we need to talk about until later. For now, let's get you home and settled. Then we'll make a plan."

Jackson's strength is what I need right now. I trust him, which is why I wanted his help with Paul. I'd be stupid to turn him away.

Please, God, help me through this. I've never felt pain like this before and I need it to stop.

Whether I like it or not, Jackson is my new roommate.

Making decisions hurts my head too much, so at this point I'm pretty much agreeable to everything he suggests. The one thing I'm grateful for is Jackson didn't insist I talk about my feelings.

I've always loved quiet time away from work, until now. Without the distractions of the job, my brain is on overload. Now, I have too much time on my hands to think. Self-doubt cripples me.

Thoughts of Kellie are the only thing keeping me from going crazy.

The way she took care of me when I needed it most. Holding her all night and listening to the soft noises she makes while sleeping. Then this morning and how it just felt right, despite my inner turmoil. Waking up to her cooking breakfast in the kitchen seemed perfectly natural at the most unnatural time. How can someone I barely know have such an effect on me?

I have so many questions to ask Kellie. The one that keeps floating around my mind; she's been mine for longer than I know. What did she mean by this?

It's still early, but I can barely keep my eyes open, so I text Kellie before I fall asleep.

Me: Hi, Kellie. I'm exhausted already. Can I call you tomorrow?

Kellie: Of course. Get some sleep and call when you can. I'll be here.

Me: TTYL. Good Night

I set my phone next to the bed and pray my overworked brain will turn off long enough for me to sleep.

The early morning sun shines through my bedroom window, waking me earlier than planned. I usually close the blackout blinds before going to sleep, but last night wasn't like every other night.

Throwing the covers off my body, I sit on the edge of the mattress and talk myself into getting out of bed. It would be easy to lie here and wallow away in grief and misery. Too easy to crawl inside the blackness I feel flowing through my veins.

"Lance, are you up yet?" Jackson speaks through my closed door.

"Yeah, I'm up."

"Come on. Let's go for a run. You're getting flabby, and we can't have that now, can we?"

"I swear to God, Jackson, you really need to work on your people skills and small talk."

"Lance, get your fucking ass out of that bedroom, right now. There, is that better?" He's laughing at me and the fucker made me smile when I want to stay in a bad mood.

"Give me a minute to take a piss and I'll be right there." I'm not mad. Without Jackson's encouragement, who knows if I would have given in to the voices telling me to stay under the covers.

There is no sense in showering. Fuck it! I'm not making the bed either. Instead, I throw on some old workout clothes and stomp downstairs.

Jackson's waiting with the front door open. "About time, let's go." Jackson's enthusiasm to work out is not mirrored by me.

"Yes sir, Deputy Asshole, sir." I'm a little cranky because who the fuck wants to run at zero dark thirty.

Allowing Jackson to set the slow, steady pace, I have a suspicion this will be a long run.

Five minutes in, I hear footsteps behind us in the otherwise silent morning. I glance over my shoulder and see Sergeant Williams and Javier running at the same pace about fifteen feet behind.

"What's this about, Jackson?"

He doesn't answer, just shrugs his shoulders, and keeps the pace moving forward.

Turning the next corner, I hear more footsteps pounding the pavement. Another peek behind me and I see at least ten more of my family of blue. It's then that I notice they all have the same T-shirt on. Navy Blue with Paul's badge number in gold.

Rounding the corner, and blocks away from my house, the number of men and women running behind Jackson and I have more than tripled. Not everyone is from the sheriff's department. EMT's, Fire, Rescue, and other first responders are here to show respect to Paul and support me. Having them all wearing matching shirts with Paul's badge is staggering.

Deep down, I know they are all here to support me, and honor Paul, but that's not what the irrational side of my brain is telling me. With every added footstep I hear a whisper, *you failed, you failed, you failed*.

I feel suffocated by the sheer number of bodies behind me. The feeling of being chased unnerves me. I feel they judge me for letting my partner down. My own crazy brain sends my flight instinct into overdrive. This isn't a race, it's my attempt to escape reality. I don't deserve or want their support after failing Paul.

As my composure dissolves, my pace increases into a full sprint. I can't let them see how vulnerable and weak I am. I pump my arms faster, leaning into the run, needing more distance from the crowd behind me. No matter how hard I try, they close in while some catch up and run alongside me.

My body tires and begins to slow, ignoring my demand to

keep going. I stumble to the edge of the grass surrounding the county park and crumble into an exhausted heap on the ground.

The quadricep muscles in my thighs twitch and burn from the strain of the run. Pain in my calves give way to almost unbearable spasms. My heart hammers inside my chest and feels like it's about to explode. A huge part of me welcomes the abuse I've put my body through as penance for my short-comings.

The grass is soft, tempting me to lie face down and ignore everyone standing around me. After catching my breath, I sit back on my heels and gaze upon the men and women who have been running with me for miles. Jackson stands front and center.

Betrayal creeps in. Jackson promised to keep people away from me and here I am surrounded. I spit out my anger. "I don't understand why you're all here. I told Jackson I want to be alone."

"Lance, you don't get it. No matter how hard you try, you can't outrun your family. We've got your back even when you try to push us away." Jackson steps forward and squats down, now at eye level with me. He offers me a T-shirt printed with 1459, now and forever Paul's badge number. "Now, put this shirt on, stand with the rest of us and let's get you home."

I'm proud to be part of my family of blue and pretend to use my old shirt to wipe sweat from my forehead, when in reality I'm scrubbing away the tears. I don't want my friends to see my despair, even though I know they would under-stand. I shouldn't worry because I turn to look at them, many openly weeping, but without the shame I feel. Paul was loved by so many and this group is only a portion of the people whose lives he's touched. He deserves to be honored and remembered. Today is just the beginning of our healing.

Jackson reaches out his hand to help me up to my feet. My

muscles are like jelly and I lean into him for support. When he pulls me into a hug, a few hands slap my back while everyone around us shouts *OORAH* in solidarity.

Taking the new shirt from Jackson. I peel off my old ratty T-shirt, slip into the new one and shout, *"OORAH Paul!"*

My body is still aching from a combination of exercise and stress. The long walk home, surrounded by friends was comforting. As we got closer to my house, the group thinned out as they reached their cars. I was so engrossed in my thoughts I never saw the vehicles while running. It's out of character for me to be so oblivious to my surroundings.

It was only Jackson and I again for the last mile.

"Thank you for putting this together."

"I wish I could take credit, but this was all Javier's idea. He called everyone and they jumped on board with the plan, no questions asked."

"The rookie did good on this one." Using the keyless entry for my front door, I enter the code and walk inside. "It still feels unreal that Paul took his own life."

"For me too. We're all going to miss him, Lance." Jackson pats my shoulder as he passes. Then he strolls toward the kitchen.

"I know, but that's no excuse for shutting everyone out." My reaction was explainable, but that doesn't make it right.

Jackson tosses me a cold bottle of water from the fridge. "I was thinking about going home for a few hours. I'll grab some takeout on the way back. Any requests?"

"I don't have an appetite. Right now, my body is screaming at me for beating the shit out of it on the run."

"Great, my choice for dinner then. A few of the guys asked if you were up to having them come by tonight."

"Actually, having them over would be good." I think of

Paul's reaction to my moping about and laugh. "Paul would kick my ass for acting like this."

"Yeah, he would. I'll text Javier and let him pass the word around." Jackson grabs his keys from the counter. "Are you going to be okay while I'm gone?"

"I'm good. It will give me a chance to call Kellie."

I make myself comfortable on the couch and press the dial button on my phone.

Damn it! Why did I have to meet the woman of my dreams, right now when things have turned to shit?

Wondering why I'm nervous, I feel a flutter in my stomach at hearing her voice.

"Hello?"

"Hi, Kellie. How are you?" I can hear a little voice in the background and know instantly it is Rory.

"Hi, Lance. Can you hang on one second?"

Though muffled, I can hear Kellie speak to Rory.

"Shhhh, Addy K is on the phone with a friend. Here's your goldfish crackers. Go sit down on the couch and I'll be right there."

"Thank you, Addy K."

I heard a rustling sound and imagined her settling down in a spot she could keep an eye on her gorgeous little girl. "Sorry, Rory and I were getting ready to watch a movie." Kellie sounds tired. I doubt she slept well on the couch either.

"If you're busy, I can call you tomorrow."

"No, it's fine. I have time, plus I really want to talk with you. How are you feeling?"

Better now I hear your voice.

"Tired. I went for a long run with friends this morning. It kicked my ass and made me feel old."

Kellie giggles. "I just thought of something. I have no idea how old you are. I guess we should find out a little more about one another."

She's not wrong. It confirms my suspicions. We've jumped into this too fast.

"Yeah, you're probably right. I'm twenty-eight. I know it's not considered polite to ask..."

Kellie cuts me off. "I'm twenty-four."

"I wish we could spend time together, getting to know one another and go on a real date but I don't know when I'll be free anytime soon. There's still so much to sort out."

"Lance. It's okay, I understand."

"Kellie, I need to know. Is it weird for you? Us? The instant chemistry between..."

"Honestly?" Another giggle and in my mind's eye, I can see Kellie smiling.

"Yeah, if I'm totally honest, this is really fast and it's a little scary, especially since I have Rory."

"It would be so different if, well, you know what I'm trying to say." *If my best friend didn't kill himself.*

"I really don't want to let my practical side take over but now we're talking about it, maybe we should take a step back and get to know each other when things settle down."

"I hate to say it, but you're right." I didn't intend on our conversation going this way. "I still need a friend, especially now."

"Above everything else, Lance, I'm here as your friend. Now tell me, how are you really feeling?"

I swallow hard. Admitting how much I'm dying inside isn't easy.

"It hurts like hell, Kellie."

"I know, Lance."

"I've never felt this kind of pain. I'm nauseous all the time. My head is throbbing, and it hurts to breathe."

"I wish I could take it all away. I hated it when people told me time heals." She took a deep breath, obviously reliving her own pain. "After Leslie died, I never thought I would ever feel the same, and I don't in many ways, but people were right. I learned to smile again, and mainly because of Rory, and when you're ready, I'll help you. Just remember, you won't get over this as fast as you might want to. Give yourself time." Kellie's words hold the truth I don't want to acknowledge right now.

"I feel like I failed him, Kellie. How will that thought ever go away?"

"I don't know." Her words are barely a whisper. I wonder if she still feels guilt from her sister's death.

"If you don't want to answer, you don't have to, but did you feel guilty about Leslie dying?"

"Yes, and I still feel it sometimes. Rory should have her momma taking care of her, not me. But I can't turn back time and keep second guessing myself or we will never move forward in life. We change the things we can and learn to accept the things we can't. Give it some time, Lance. I'll be here for you, I promise." Kellie sounds confident I will get past this and learn to live without Paul around, but it's too early for me to believe it.

"Thank you for being here for me now."

Comfortable silence hangs between us until Rory becomes impatient, wanting Kellie to watch the movie.

"Lance, I have to go. I promised Rory we'd make a living room fort for movie night. Will you call me tomorrow?"

"I'll call, but only if you promise I get an invite to the next movie night."

"Well, if you know how to make a fort with pillows and bedsheets, I suppose you can join us." Kellie's teasing fixes one of the cracks in my heart.

"Challenge accepted."

"Then it's a date. Oops, gotta go, Rory is trying to put up the blankets by herself."

"Good night, Kellie. I'll call you tomorrow. Enjoy your movie night."

Finally, something I can look forward to, a date with Kellie soon.

14

KELLIE

Movie night with Rory was a success. Thirty minutes into *Peter Pan* and she was fast asleep. I decide to leave her snuggled amongst the pile of pillows inside our fort for a little longer before moving her to her room.

Seeing her snuggle up with Mr. Deputy Bear warms my heart. Before now it used to bring back memories of Leslie's death, but now all I can see is Lance's smile. The same one I saw at Heath's and the one I want to try to help him find again.

I take this quiet time to tidy up around the house and allow my mind to drift back to the call with Lance. I wouldn't have guessed he was only twenty-eight. He seems mature beyond his years. I would have guessed early thirties. He wasn't trying to get me into bed, plus, he has a stable job that would be difficult to handle at the best of times, yet he didn't complain about it. He's not self-centered either and cares about others.

Anyway, his age doesn't really matter, but it highlights pieces of our lives we still need to share with each other.

"Oof." I groan when picking up Rory. It amazes me how fast she's growing. I walk slowly down the hallway, trying not to wake her. As I lean down to place her in bed, she opens her sleepy eyes and whispers the sweetest words. "I love you, Addy K."

I brush her hair away from her face, kiss her forehead lightly and say, "I love you more, baby."

Tuesday morning is just another day in the life of a single parent. First Rory woke crying and pulling on her ears. She suffers from recurring ear infections. I know the signs immediately. After calling Dr. Michaelson's office, Gloria said to bring her in.

My usually agreeable, happy niece became a monster. She didn't want to put clean clothes on, fought with me about getting in her booster seat, then threw up on me while I was carrying her into the pharmacy to pick up her medication.

It's in these moments I wish I had a partner to help. Someone who can carry Rory to bed and return to take care of me for a change. I know I can always call my parents, but I try to not lean on them for everything. This is just part of having Rory in my life. I'm sure someday I'll look back on this and laugh, but not today.

The chaos from today also reminds me how lucky I am to work from home. My boss, Aaron, is one of the most understanding men I've met. When I applied for the administrative assistant position at C & A Graphic Designs, I told him about the situation with Rory. He insisted I do as much from home as possible, only coming in when necessary. He and his wife Claire started the business a year earlier and have small children at home, so they know how hard it can be. The office is mainly set up for important client meetings. They seem happy with my performance and I don't have to stress about leaving the house every day.

Rory's fever has dropped and she's resting on the couch

watching cartoons, sipping from a juice box. I suspect the medication will kick in soon and she'll be asleep, giving me time to catch up on emails.

Booting up my laptop, I grab a banana from the fruit basket and turn on my phone to check for messages. I catch myself smiling when I see a missed call and text from Lance. It looks like he called while I was driving home about two hours ago.

Lance: Good Morning Beautiful. I hope your day is going well. I'll try to call you again later.

Oh, if he only knew what today was like.

Me: Good Afternoon. Today has been crazy. Rory's not feeling well. How are you?

I scan my emails when my cell rings. It's Lance.

"Hi."

"What's wrong with Rory? Is she okay?" There's panic in his voice.

"It's just an ear infection. She gets them a few times a year. Rory will be fine once the antibiotics kick in."

"Oh, good. Is there anything you need, or I can help with?"

"Thanks, but no. We're all set." I peek at her over the back of the couch. "In fact, she's down for the count. I'll probably have to wake her up in a few hours for her next dose of medicine."

"Well, if you need anything, call me."

My heart skips a beat. I think I just fell for Lance a little more. His concern for Rory and me is another reason he seems to be the perfect man for us.

"I will. Now tell me, how are you doing?"

I hear Lance blow out a long breath before he answers. "I had to drop off my dress uniform at the cleaners and help with a few arrangements for Paul's service on Friday. We only wear it for formal occasions like graduation, promotions, or like now, a funeral. I didn't know there was so much to do."

"Today sounds like it's been tough. Is there anything you need help with?"

"Umm, actually. I was going to ask if you would come to Paul's funeral with me, but since Rory is sick, I don't want to bother you."

"Of course, I'll be there for you, Lance. Rory can stay with my parents, but she will be good as new by Friday anyway."

"Are you sure? I don't want to impose, but I could really use some support from a *friend*." His emphasizing of the word friend reminds me of our take it slow conversation.

"I'm positive. What kind of friend would I be if I weren't there for you?"

"Thanks. It means a lot having you with me. I imagine you know what it feels like having someone important in your life die suddenly."

"You're right, I do know how much it hurts and how lonely it can feel without someone to lean on. I'll be there. Do you have the time and place?"

"We don't have the time set yet. It's scheduled for this Friday at Duggin's Funeral Home on Oak Street."

"Okay, I'll call my mom now and ask her to take Rory Thursday night and Friday. Shoot, they'll probably want her all weekend."

"Sounds good and don't forget...if you or Rory need anything, call me."

"I will and same goes for you."

"Well, I better get back to making calls. Thanks, Kellie. I'll text you once I have the time set."

"Okay. Bye, Lance."

I end the call and dial my mom's number to ask about taking Rory for the weekend. Making a pot of coffee, I settle down on my big comfy chair. This conversation may take a while since she's going to ask where I'm going, who with, and that will lead to even more questions.

"Hey, Mom. Got a minute?"

"I always have time for you, Kellie. What's going on?"

"Well, first, Rory has another ear infection. She's asleep. You know the routine. Second I need to know if you and Dad can take her Thursday night and keep her right through the weekend." I cut out the middleman and just extend her stay now since I know that will be the next thing she'll ask.

"Of course, Rory can stay with us. Not that you need a reason but what do you have going on this weekend?" Mom doesn't mean to be nosey, but she does like to stay on top of things.

"I have a funeral to attend with a friend and just figured it would be easier to have Rory stay the weekend with you than worry about running back and forth." I intentionally leave out Lance's name or any details since there is nothing to share. Technically he is just a friend, even if he's the man I want to share a bigger part of my life with.

"Oh, Kellie, I'm so sorry. Is it someone I know?"

"It's no one you know." Before my mom can ask any more questions, I continue. "Thanks, Mom, I'll drop Rory off on Thursday, but I need to get back to work before she wakes up."

"Plan on staying for dinner and give my angel a kiss from Gram Gram and Grumpa. I'll call tonight and check on you two. Talk to you later."

"Okay, bye, Mom." I end the call and sit back in the chair. I'm glad Lance asked me to accompany him, but I'm worried about how he will handle these three days leading up to the funeral. I remember everything we had to do for Leslie. Planning and sorting through the funeral and burial process can be agonizing.

I send Jackson a text to remind him I'm here to help if they need it.

Me: Hey Jackson, it's Kellie. Just checking in. Don't forget if you or Lance need anything don't hesitate to call me. Lance asked me to come Friday to the services, so I'll see you there.

Jackson: Thanks Kellie. For everything. I'll see you Friday then.

Me: See you Friday.

15

LANCE

The Springhill Sheriff's Department is following the same protocol for Paul's death, just as they would any fallen officer. As is custom, everyone will wear black ribbon across their badge to represent mourning. In the past few years, I've worn the band, but this time its meaning is deeply personal.

Losing one of our own is always hard, but our agency has never had to deal with a co-worker committing suicide.

Jackson is still a guest at my house and is the only person I feel comfortable leaning on for support. Even that isn't easy. I do my best to hold myself together in front of everyone but him because I allow him to see my damaged side. He doesn't judge me when I vent my frustrations and release some of the pain that never seems to completely stop tormenting me.

As agreed, I text Kellie the details for the funeral and told her I'd pick her up at noon. We've only talked a few times these past few days because I had a lot to do. But if I'm being totally honest busying myself was my excuse not to confide in her and expose how bad my mental state is.

My further decline into hell started when my buddies visited. I'd play the host and hand out beers while sharing our favorite memories of Paul. We'd all raise a toast to him.

While their support is appreciated, I hate hearing them talk about what a great guy Paul *was*. In their minds, he is already part of their past, but I can't let go of him, not yet.

All I want to do is scream about him being a selfish asshole, a coward who couldn't stand up and admit he needed help. How I hated him for not trusting me to be there to support him. Then disgusted with myself for having such horrible thoughts about a dead man who can't defend himself any longer, guilt would eat me alive.

When it was Jackson and me, I'd bring out the whiskey, slamming back shots until reality slipped from my mind. I used alcohol to fool my brain into thinking Paul might still be alive and playing another stupid prank. I told myself it couldn't be real, and Paul would be here pounding on my door before work because I was running late again. Of course, morning would come, and reality would sucker punch me in the gut. It became a vicious cycle. Jackson was the one who pointed out the path I was spiraling down. Without him, I wouldn't have survived.

Drinking alone, I offer a toast, laced with anger and bitterness. "Here's to Paul. You were the best friend and partner a man could ever have." Raising my glass high, I spill some of the alcohol from the over filled glass. Not giving a shit how much I've already had to drink, I bring the glass to my lips, tip my head back, and pour the amber liquid down my throat. The slow burn I felt on the first three shots is non-existent now. A sign that my plan to forget is working.

Jackson tries to reason with me. "Lance. Drinking yourself into a stupor every night isn't going to change the fact Paul is gone." Just like last night, Jackson is sitting across the dining table from me, watching as I self-medicate with booze. He tries reassuring me I'm not the one to blame, but I refuse to accept it.

"Fuck you, Jackson. Just, fuck you." Anger spills from me like bile. "He wasn't your partner, was he? No! He was mine and I failed him. I was supposed to have his back. It was my job." I throw the shot glass against the wall, watching it shatter on impact. "Just go home and leave me alone." Swiping the half empty bottle from the table, I stand and walk outside to the patio and flop down on the deck chair.

Jackson trails behind and sits beside me. I glance over where he's kicked back, staring up into the night sky.

"Why didn't he talk to me?" He remains silent, letting me ramble on. "What made him think this was his only option? Why didn't he trust me to help?" My voice is hoarse while I work to hold back the anger I feel. These questions are on a loop in my head demanding answers which will never come. I don't try to stop the tears I held back all day. I can't do it. Jackson has cried along with me and I know, if I look over to him now, his eyes will be filled with tears.

Jackson blows out an exasperated breath and replies, "Lance, you know I can't answer those questions. None of us can. Paul made the choice to take his life and now we are left to pick up the pieces. But as much as you fight me. I will not sit by while you self-destruct."

Unscrewing the top from the bottle, I chug more whiskey and throw it against the wooden fence. I'm still conscious so I debate returning to the house for more liquor.

"Just fucking go, Jackson. Come back tomorrow if you want, but right now I want to be alone."

"Not gonna happen, man. Listen to what you're asking me. I'm not leaving. You need to trust me, just as you asked of Paul. Well, now it's your turn. I'm here and I'll be here tomorrow and the next day, and the next day after that. Got it?" Even in my drunken state, I recognize the smooth and matter of fact tone Jackson uses when speaking to me.

"I'm not sure what to do. I do trust you. I just don't trust myself right now." I slump back into the chair cushion, giving in to the fog that's finally begun to take over from the alcohol.

"We'll figure this out. Just know, you don't have to do this by yourself." Jackson stands, pats my shoulder, and walks back towards the house.

"What the fuck, Jackson? You're leaving?" After that speech, I'm shocked he's walking away.

"Nah, man, just making some coffee. I have a feeling it's going to be another long night and tomorrow's wake is going to be difficult enough without a hangover."

Kellie did not attend the wake with me on Thursday evening because I didn't ask her to. Although having her by my side would have been comforting, this part is mainly for family and close friends to pay their respects privately. This is a much smaller gathering than is expected tomorrow. We have had to move Friday's memorial service to St. Anthony's to accommodate the masses of family, friends and colleagues wanting to say their goodbyes. Although Paul was not religious, an exception was made, allowing the Sheriff's department to use their church for the funeral.

I can't bear to leave my partner alone and arrive early, choosing to sit in the front pew. My eyes rarely leave the flag draped coffin. A large frame holding an arrangement of white roses stands beside a framed photograph of Paul in the dress uniform we will all wear tomorrow.

Inside the small chapel, our agency's honor guard stands watch over Paul's body. They have been with him all day, rotating out every thirty minutes, saluting him, before marching slowly past the pews. Each time they change guard, my heart thuds heavy in my chest. The respect shown to my brother as he lay in his casket brings on a wave of emotion I never imagined possible.

Nobody speaks above a whisper when entering the chapel. A sign of the cross, salute or head nod is all that is necessary. The quiet of the day is welcomed, allowing me to mourn for my best friend in peace.

Jackson walks from the back and sits beside me, reminding me to take a break.

"Lance. I will sit with Paul while you go for a walk. There is water and a plate of food for you in the waiting area."

"I can't leave him alone." I barely choke out the words.

"Which is understandable and why I said I'll stay until you return. Now, go eat something."

"You're right." I stand, walk to Paul's casket, and salute him. Turning sharply on my heel, I follow the same path down the aisle as the guards and past the watch commander standing at the entry way.

Driving to pick up Kellie, I work myself up into an anxiety attack. My appetite has been shit but I forced down some coffee and toast after a long run early this morning. Unable to keep my meager breakfast down, I pull to the side of the road and empty the contents of my stomach.

With the engine running, I sit on the shoulder, desperately fighting to keep control. At least for today.

After checking behind me for other cars, I shift into drive, and turn up the radio to drown out the angry voices still running through my head. Unfortunately, the country song playing through the car speakers is about finding out who your friends are. It's impossible to ignore what I know to be true.

Don't pretend like you didn't play a part in Paul's death. You sat next to him daily. Heard his worries and did nothing. When he complained about the job being too stressful, you never asked what he was really saying. Paul was screaming inside for help and you took your time to get it for him. You failed.

"Shut the fuck up!" I'm not sure if I'm screaming at the

radio or the voices in my head but they both need to be silent before I arrive at Kellie's.

I turn the radio off, then bang my palm against the steering wheel.

Arriving at Kellie's, I turn off the engine, place my hat on my head and walk up to her door.

Kellie opens it before I have a chance to knock. She's wearing a navy colored, knee length, sheath dress with black heels. Ironically, it matches my uniform in color. Her deep auburn hair is down, brushing her shoulders.

"You look beautiful, Kellie."

"And you are the most handsome man I've ever met, Lance."

"Thank you." I run my hands nervously over the heavy, wool coat.

"I didn't expect you to wear a formal uniform today. You look different."

"Is that a bad thing?"

"Not at all, Lance. You look very distinguished."

"Thanks. I think the last time I wore my dress uniform was over a year ago at the promotion ceremony. Are you ready?"

"I am." Kellie pulls her front door closed and accepts my outstretched hand.

"I'm glad you're with me, Kellie." I open the truck door and help her inside. "I can't tell you how much it means to me."

"It's what friends do, Lance." She grins shyly and adds. "I'll support you as long as you need me to"

The number of police vehicles and uniformed first responders from local agencies attending today is overwhelming. I look around at the sea of officers standing near the church entrance waiting for the service to start. Men and women who never met Paul but are now here to honor and pay their respects.

"Lance, we need to go inside now." Kellie links her fingers through mine.

"Okay."

When I don't move, Kellie turns to face me, gently placing her palm on the side of my face. I close my eyes and lean into her touch.

"Come on, Lance. I won't leave your side. Jackson is waiting for us. The others won't enter until you are inside."

Looking towards the church, I see Jackson at the top of the stairs.

"Alright." I take Kellie's hand, drape it over the crook of my elbow and walk past the others to the large wooden doors.

"Are you ready?" Jackson asks.

I swallow down the lump in my throat and nod.

Jackson opens the door and I walk through, pulling Kellie close to my side. I'm not sure I would be able to stand, let alone make my way to the front pew without her support.

"Lance, you and Kellie will sit here." Jackson gestures to the bench to the left of the alter, across the aisle from where Paul's family is already seated. The casket will be brought in by the honor guard after everyone is settled.

Kellie sits first, leaving me space next to the aisle.

"Thanks, Jackson."

"I'll be sitting right behind you once everyone has taken their seats. I need to let Sergeant Williams know those standing outside can enter now." Jackson's voice echoes around the quiet of the sanctuary.

I let my mind wander through most of the service, but not once did I take my eyes off the flag covered casket. It is closed but I know what Paul is wearing for the final journey to his resting place; the same uniform I have on now. Not wanting to picture his face and what he looked like after the shooting and later in the hospital, I work to replace sad times with memories of happier ones. Images from Paul and Jane's wedding fill my thoughts. I want to imagine they are together in the afterlife, as they always should be. Soulmates reconnected and Paul's shattered heart finally healed.

When the time comes for me to speak to the congregation, I hesitate. Whispering to Kellie, I'm terrified I won't be able to finish what I want to say. "Kellie, will you come up with me?"

"Of course." Kellie takes my hand in hers.

Standing, she slips her arm through mine. A deep cough from the back of the room breaks the silence while we walk up the steps to the alter and position ourselves behind a podium. The microphone picks up the sound of me clearing my throat. I look to Kellie who has taken a step back from where I stand. She lifts a white handkerchief to her eyes and dabs away a tear before it falls down her cheek. My heart skips when I recognize the monogram.

L M

16

KELLIE

Standing at the altar, just to the left of Lance, I feel a little scared facing a room full of strangers. To stop my knees knocking together, I lock them and focus my attention on the man grieving the loss of his best friend. Seeing his strained profile, I know the agony and turmoil he feels inside only too well. When he turns to look at me over his shoulder, my heart breaks for him. For Lance and those left behind, experience tells me this is only the start of the grieving process. The angst in his eyes chips away the armor I've worn all day.

At times of great sadness, tears will fall and right now, the collective emotion felt in this holy place brings a wave of my own tears. All I can do is surrender to my emotions, let the tears fall and wipe them away with the handkerchief Lance gave me the day we met. I doubt he remembers telling me to keep it.

"Good Afternoon. My name is Deputy Lance Malloy. Thank you all for being here today to celebrate the life of Deputy Paul Lancaster. He was my partner and the best friend I could ever have." He looks up to the vaulted ceiling, struggling to finish what I know he needs to say. "I'm sorry. It was much easier writing these words than speaking them.

Please bear with me." I place my hand on his back, just so he remembers I'm still there for him. "I never expected to be saying goodbye to my partner today." Lance clears his throat and continues. "Paul and I met on our first day at the academy, where we bonded over our inability to beat the demon obstacle course. The day we completed the graduation requirement, shaving off over three minutes from our best time, we celebrated until the sun came up. Sleep deprived and hungover, we arrived in class disheveled and smelling of stale booze. This did not slip by the drill instructor's eagle eyes and as punishment, a surprise ten-mile run was added to the start of the day. We weren't the most popular recruits that morning, but we both agreed it was worth it and wouldn't have changed a thing."

Lance turns over the paper he's reading from and continues sharing his thoughts.

"Having Paul as a partner was never dull. Like the night we were called to help rescue a cat which was stuck under a house with its kittens. Paul decided I should be the one to investigate. After removing my duty belt and prying off the metal grate, I crawled into the tight space, then flat on my belly, reached in to pull them to safety. Unfortunately, the loud cries were not from a black cat but an incredibly angry and protective momma skunk. She sprayed me full on before I could escape. When I finally squeezed out from under the elderly woman's house, Paul's howling laughter brought out the nearby neighbors. The homeowner insisted tomato juice was the first step in removing the awful smell and poured several bottles over my head before Paul hosed me down with freezing water. A few months later, I was able to get even when we were dispatched to deal with an attempted assault on multiple parties at the local park. As it turns out, the assailant was an aggressive goose, nipping and biting park visitors and animal control was not readily available." A ripple of laughter brings a little light to this dark, solemn occasion. "Even Paul agreed, the recording of him chasing the crazy goose was fair payback and these incidents are just two of the strangest calls we encountered together while on the job."

Looking out into the sea of faces, I observe smiles and hear more lighthearted chuckles. Lance's silly stories makes me wish I'd had the opportunity to meet Paul at Heath's last week.

"I could go on for hours telling stories about how Paul deserves his hero status. For instance, the day we were called to the grocery store to help a single mother seen crying in her vehicle for over an hour."

I could tell by the rise and fall in his voice Lance was struggling to get through his speech. Memories can bring much happiness but can also overwhelm.

"When we approached her, she was counting out pennies and sorting through coupons scattered on the passenger seat. Paul listened as the lady explained why she was so distraught. She'd been laid off and with her savings account empty, she was desperately trying to find a way to feed her children. Those of us who knew Paul, knew how big his heart was."

I looked out and saw heads nodding in agreement with Lance's comment.

"He walked the aisles, filling a cart with enough groceries to last a month. Two weeks later, Paul and I stopped by her home for a follow up. Her smile was bright. She had hope because she'd found a new job. Apparently, a few days after Paul purchased her groceries, the store manager called her out of the blue offering an interview for the open position in their administrative offices. When I side eyed Paul, his feigned innocence was worthy of an Oscar. I tried to bring it up later that day, but Paul brushed me off. That was so typical of him, never wanting to take credit for his good deeds. He just saw it as part of the job."

Before continuing, Lance looks to me with fear in his eyes. A silent cry for help I can't ignore. Stepping forward, I take hold of his hand, using my touch to convey support to the man I'm falling in love with.

"I'm here," I whisper. "You can do this Lance." Keeping my voice low and hoping the microphone won't pick up my words, I encourage him to continue.

"My best friend crumbled after his wife died. Two people destined to be together forever and it's no excuse, but Paul loved Jane with every fiber of his being and couldn't bear to be apart from her. She was Juliette to his Romeo. Their love story is the kind romance authors dream of writing. Watching Jane deteriorate as cancer took hold destroyed him. I knew he was hurting. I just didn't know how much. The only consolation I cling to in this moment is that they are together again, slow dancing under the stars just as they did on their first date. That is how I choose to remember Paul. Happy and in the arms of his one true love." He swallows hard and stands a little taller. "Rest in peace my friend. Until we meet again."

Lance turns away from the podium with unshed tears filling his eyes. If only I could find a way to help ease some of his pain.

Walking down the steps, hand in hand with Lance, the opening lines of *Why* by *Rascal Flatt's* fills the silence. The words couldn't be more apt. I have no doubt in my mind, Paul was a troubled soul who didn't realize life was worth fighting for.

Sitting beside Lance in his truck, I follow his lead and stay silent. The church service was difficult, and my gut is saying the graveside committal will be harder still. We join the funeral procession, keeping a respectable distance behind the lead car which transports Paul's family to the cemetery. The line of cars stretching behind us is so long, I can't see where it ends.

We drive through the tall iron gates and park beside rows of grave markers. With the windows down, I can smell the fresh cut grass and feel the cool breeze. Lance stares straight ahead, making no attempt to leave his truck.

"Are you okay, Lance?"

"Yeah. Um, hang on. Let me come around and help you out." He turns off the engine, steps out and heads to my side of the truck. Even at his lowest he still thinks of me.

We walk across the grass in a straight path between granite headstones to the open grave. Just as we did in the church, Lance and I sit in chairs beside Paul's parents. There is only a makeshift aisle between us. The crowd of funeral attendees begin to form a circle, leaving an opening for the honor guard to carry the casket to Paul's final resting place.

Pipers play the familiar melody, *Going Home*, on bagpipes as the flag draped casket is carried effortlessly by the guard before coming to rest in front of us. The music softly drifts away in the breeze as an eerie calm falls upon the hallowed grounds.

"Please stand." The police chaplain begins the committal prayers. "My name is Chaplin Geoffrey Robertson of the Springhill Deputy Sheriff's Association. On behalf of Deputy Paul Lancaster's family, I would like to thank all of you for joining us here today. Though Paul leaves behind family and friends, their hearts shattered by his sad passing, he would want us to find a way through the hurt and anger we collectively feel and find a way to remember him in happy times. We may never know the reasons why but take comfort in the knowledge he has gone on to a better place-reunited, at last, with the love of his life, Jane. As she finds herself in Paul's arms once more, we are left behind, struggling to find a way to move forward without him in our lives. Grieving will take much longer than you want, or feel is fair because losing such an amazing man will always leave a gaping hole in our hearts. I implore you to reach out to one another in your time of grief. Hold each other up. Say a kind word, offer to listen, show love and be kind. Only then Paul's death will not have been in vain. If we take one thing away from this tragedy let it be this... You are never alone. Rest in Peace Deputy Lancaster."

The chaplain's words hang heavy in the air as the priest who spoke at the church offers his own words of comfort. "Heavenly Father, please give us the strength to leave Paul in your care. Welcome him home with open arms and surround him with love. His passing is a great shock to all of us, but his death serves as a reminder that we live in an imperfect world and of mankind's failings, flaws, and limitations. Standing here, we mourn the death of our family member, friend and colleague. Take solace in the knowledge there is no isolation in heaven. We can rest easy knowing Paul and Jane have been reunited and that we will not be separated from our loved ones forever. We too will one day meet again, as heaven is a perpetual reunion."

Jackson marches in front of us, followed by an officer carrying a bugle under his arm. They stand beside the chaplain. Raising the instrument to his lips, the heartbreaking sounds of Taps begins while the guards lift the flag from the casket, folding the corners sharply into a triangle. With the ends of the flag tucked firmly into place, an officer presents it to Jackson, salutes and returns to formation. The bugler has finished playing his final call and stands at attention.

A mournful wail pierces the silence, drawing my attention away from Jackson to Paul's mother who is clinging desperately to her husband's coat sleeve. A flash of Leslie's burial and Rory in my arms has me reaching for Lance, sliding my hand into his. Today has brought back a few of the bad memories I've forced from my mind, but it's not the time to deal with my problems. I'm here for Lance.

Kneeling before Paul's mother, Jackson holds the flag between his palms. "Mrs. Lancaster, please accept this flag as a symbol of our appreciation for your son's honorable and faithful service."

I gasp for breath as Paul's mother takes the flag and clutches it tightly against her heaving chest. Jackson marches past us, eyes forward the entire time. The priest offers a final blessing before closing the service. "The Lancaster family would like to thank you for coming today. There will be a reception to celebrate Paul's extraordinary life at the Deputy Sheriff's Association hall. Before you leave, I would like to pray for each of you." A moment's pause follows. "Dear Lord, I ask for courage. Courage for these men and women to face and conquer their fears. I ask for strength of body and mind while they serve the community they are prepared to protect with their last breath. I ask for compassion, concern, and trust to be given and accepted by all. And please Lord, do all of this while standing by their side. Amen."

17

LANCE

As the others walk in silence to their vehicles, Paul's parents, Kellie, and I stay behind to have our own private moment graveside. Tenderly brushing her fingers over the smooth mahogany casket, Paul's mother weeps and falls into her husband's arms. His father's stoic façade has disappeared, leaving behind a grief-stricken parent in its wake.

"Do you mind if I speak with the Lancaster's before we leave?"

"Of course, I don't mind, Lance." She gives me an understanding look. "Why don't I wait by your truck while you have some time with Paul as well." Kellie's kindness and strength grounds me, holding me in place throughout today's services.

"Thank you." I hand her my keys. "Don't stand in the hot sun–there is air conditioning in the cab."

The thought of one last goodbye has my stomach churning again, but I know if I don't take this time with Paul, I will hold onto regret for a lifetime.

She takes the keys from me. "Take as long as you need, Lance. There's no rush." Kellie lifts her hand to my cheek. Using her thumb, she gently brushes away a stray tear I didn't know was there. I've cried so much this week I barely notice anymore. Her touch takes away some of the hurt coursing through my body.

Kellie walks away, giving me space to say what I need to say.

Watching and waiting for my turn, I witness Paul's mother and father kiss the top of the casket. This is their last gesture of love to the child they will grieve an eternity for. As they turn to walk away, I stop them to extend my condolences again.

"Mr. and Mrs. Lancaster. Would you mind if I took a moment of your time?"

"Of course not, Lance," Mr. Lancaster replies.

"I can't tell you how much Paul meant to me." *Take it slow, Lance.* "He was much more than a partner and I'll miss him every day." Mrs. Lancaster stifles a sob. "I wish I could turn back time and protect him before he..." My throat tightens. "I'm so sorry." My heart pounds, the pain in my chest almost overwhelming.

When Mrs. Lancaster looks to me, I see the dark circles under her eyes from lack of sleep. She wipes at her tears and levels me with a stare of what looks like concern.

"Lance, we are not angry with you. We love you as if you were one of our own." She reaches for my hand. "You're tearing yourself apart, but this is not your fault. We missed the signs as well, and our guilt will never bring Paul back to us." She takes in a deep cleansing breath. I hold onto her hand, wishing I could take her own hurt away.

Mr. Lancaster adds, "Paul loved you like a brother and we don't blame you. Our son made the decision to end his life." His words choked him. "You were the one who stayed by his side throughout Jane's illness when others moved on. Nobody could ask for a better friend and if you ever need anything at all, please don't hesitate to call us. Day or night. Okay?"

"Yes, sir." I dip my chin low in shame. I want to agree with them but can't seem to look past my mistakes.

"We love you, Lance. Spend time with Paul but don't linger too long. This is not how he wants us to remember him." Mrs. Lancaster pulls me into a motherly hug, providing some relief to my aching heart.

The only sound I hear is the rustling of leaves from the large oak trees lining the walkway.

I've already said goodbye in my head a hundred times. Logic tells me this is just a body and Mrs. Lancaster is right, standing here alone, berating myself won't change anything. Paul would want me to make it quick, move on with my life. It's not going to be a swift change, but I'll try.

"I'm so mad at you I could scream. I just don't understand. We talked about everything. Why couldn't you tell me how bad things really were? Why didn't you let me help?" Getting angry won't give me the answers I seek but allows me to release my frustration. But, this is not how I want my last moments with Paul to be. "I still need you. You left me behind to try and live my life without you in it." I can feel anger rising and swallow it back. "I know in time the pain I feel will fade, but I'll never forget you. I want you to know I forgive you. Give Jane a hug and kiss from me. I don't plan on seeing you soon, but eventually we will be reunited. Save a seat for me partner. Goodbye my friend, until we meet again."

I kiss my fingertips and brush them over the top of the casket.

Turning to leave, I see Kellie standing beside my truck. Instead of waiting in the cab for me, she meets me halfway and leads me to where everyone is gathered around Sergeant Williams' vehicle.

There is one final piece to the funeral proceeding. Paul's End of Watch call over the radio from dispatch. Knowing how important this is, my family of blue waited for me before starting.

"Are you ready?" Although surrounded by hundred's, he speaks directly to me.

"Yes, Sir." I struggle to bring air into my lungs. There is no way to be ready for the words about to be spoken.

Reaching into his squad car, Sarge removes the mic. "I-1751 to dispatch. Check status of Squad-1459."

A squelch of the radio is followed by a dispatcher calling for Paul to respond to his radio.

"Dispatch to Squad-1459." The dispatcher pauses, waiting for Paul to return her request for a status check.

I close my eyes and picture Paul sitting beside me in our squad car as he replies with 10-8, letting her know that we are in service and ready to take a call.

"Dispatch to Squad-1459." With still no answer from my partner, she continues. "Deputy Paul Lancaster, badge number 1459 to dispatch…" She breaks off, as if waiting for a miracle. "I-1751, no response from Squad-1459."

Sergeant Williams replies to dispatch, removing Paul from service for the last time. "10-4 dispatch, show Squad-1459 as 10-7, out of service."

Kellie wraps her arms around my waist. I look down and see a stream of tears flowing freely down her cheeks. Pulling her tight against my body, I hold my breath and wait for Paul's end of watch to be announced.

"All units please be advised, Squad-1459 is 10-7." The dispatcher takes a deep breath. "It is with great sorrow, we mourn the passing of Deputy Paul Lancaster, badge number 1459. End of watch on June 10th 08:34am. Gone but never forgotten. Deputy Lancaster, we consider it an honor to have served with you. Your brothers and sisters in blue will watch over your family. May you rest in eternal peace, Deputy. We have the watch from here."

My head feels like it's trapped in a vice. Pressure from the dull headache I've had for hours continues to increase the closer we get to Kellie's house.

"Are you okay, Lance? You're quiet."

"I have a slight headache, but I'll be fine. I'm only glad today is finally over."

We arrive at Kellie's house. I put the truck in park and shut the engine off. Rubbing my forehead, hoping to find some relief, I confess how I really feel. "I've never felt so drained of emotion like this in my entire life. If not for this headache, I'd feel nothing."

Stepping out of the truck, I walk around to open the passenger door. Kellie accepts my hand and doesn't let go.

"Come inside. I'll get you something for your head and cook us dinner."

"Are you sure? I don't want to be a bother." Food is the last thing I want, but the chance to spend more time with Kellie overrules my lack of appetite.

"It's nothing fancy, just left-over pot roast and veggies." She opens the front door and turns to me with a sympathetic smile. "Come on, follow me into the kitchen and I'll get us both fed."

She doesn't wait for me to answer and leaves the door open for me to follow her inside.

The living room is as I remember it from the night Paul died. Bins of toys and books against the wall, a reminder that Kellie has Rory to care for, yet tonight she's caring for me instead.

From the kitchen, Kellie calls out to me. "What do you want to drink? I have apple juice, *Dr. Pepper*, or water."

Following her voice, I turn the corner into the kitchen and freeze. Kellie is bent over, searching through the refrigerator, giving me a perfect view of her shapely ass. Briefly, I consider stepping forward, spinning her around and claiming her lips with soft but passionate kisses.

"Lance? What can I get you to drink?" Kellie's repeated question halts the direction my thoughts were travelling down. We decided to remain friends for now and take it slow. Both agreeing we have a lot we still need to know about each other before moving out of the friendzone and into something intimate. But try telling that to my brain when the woman in front of me has turned out to be everything I dream of.

"Water would be great."

Kellie takes a bottle from the shelf and passes it to me. She reaches into the fridge again and removes a large foil covered roasting pan.

"Let me help." Placing my water on the counter, I take the leftovers from her and place it on top of the stove.

"Thanks! Hang on, let me get you something for your headache from the medicine cabinet in the bathroom." She returns quickly to the kitchen and places two tablets in the palm of my hand. "Why don't you sit down. It will only take a minute to warm this up in the microwave." She dishes up two plates of pot roast, potatoes and carrots then heats them one at a time.

Too tired to object, I take the pills with a swallow of water. Once the food is ready, Kellie brings the hot plates to the table. I stand and pull out a chair across from me for Kellie to sit.

"Like I said, nothing fancy but I hope you like it."

"It smells delicious. Thank you." The savory aroma of the meal has my mouth watering. My appetite seems to have returned and I dig in with gusto. The intensity of the headache has reduced significantly. I suspect it's more from shutting off my brain, than taking the pills.

After eating almost half the food from my plate, I notice the placemat with the picture of canine astronauts and the plastic booster seat in the chair beside Kellie. "So, unless you're a fan of the movie, *Space Dogs*, I'm guessing that is Rory's seat."

"Oh, I'm definitely a fan of that movie, but yes, that is Rory's spot." Kellie shakes pepper onto her potatoes. "She goes through phases of what she likes based on the movies we watch and books we read. We've just finished Treasure Island and have started reading about the knights of the round table."

"I remember seeing that book last week on your living room table. Would you like to know a secret?" She nods and I lean in close to whisper. "Okay, but no telling. Not many outside of my family knows, but my first name is actually Lancelot."

"No way, Lance, you're pulling my leg."

My desire for Kellie to know more about my life has me sharing a secret very few people know. I've tried my best to keep it to myself since grade school. Once the other kids found out my given name, the teasing became unbearable. My parents agreed to shorten my name to Lance. They also asked the teachers to use my chosen name. It took a few years before everyone forgot and moved on to the next unfortunate kid to harass.

"I'd like to say I'm joking, but it's one hundred percent true. My parents were slightly obsessed with the knights and even read passages from the classic novel, Le Morte d'Arthur, during their wedding ceremony." I take another bite of the roast and hum my appreciation. "This is delicious. I'm hungrier than I thought."

"I'm glad you like it. So, what's La Mot Da Author?" She giggles when destroying the title of the book.

"You're killing me." It's my turn to laugh. "It's pronounced, Le Morte d'Arthur. The books are the full telling of the Arthurian legend. Starting with King Arthur's birth, it continues all the way until his death. Each knight has their

171

own book and Sir Lancelot is their favorite. I was named before I was ever conceived."

"So, what makes Lancelot so special your parents would want to name their son after him?"

"Lancelot was known to be a brave, noble and honorable man. However, he had a dark side." Kellie's eyes widen. "He betrays his friend, King Arthur, by sleeping with Queen Guinevere. Shame and guilt over his sins, he leaves the kingdom, but always remained loyal to his King. Years later, when Arthur's ill-conceived son, Mordred, attempts to take over the throne, Lancelot returns to fight. Arthur and Lancelot battle alongside each other and their friendship is restored."

"Wow. You know a lot about this don't you. Brave, noble, and honorable. I completely agree with that description of you."

"I'm not so sure about that."

"Well I'm sure and nothing you say will convince me of anything different, so don't even try. Now tell me how you know so much about Lancelot?"

"My dad loved to tell me stories on the rare occasions he was home before my bedtime. I loved those nights and would battle to stay awake just so he would keep talking. Those are some of my favorite childhood memories."

"I love reading to Rory at bedtime. I'd be heartbroken if I missed out on snuggle time. Why was it rare for your father to be home?"

"Just part of the job. My dad is a retired lieutenant from Guerneville Police Department. He worked the midnight shift a lot when I was young. I guess it prepared me for when I'm assigned the same crazy schedule."

"I think it's wonderful you've followed in your father's footsteps. I'm sure if he had been given the choice, he would have been with you every night." She gestures to my empty plate. "Would you like more roast?"

"I'm stuffed but thank you anyway." I pick up both plates and carry them to the sink.

Turning on the hot water, I squeeze dish soap onto the yellow sponge and begin washing them.

"Lance, you don't have to do that. Scoot over and let me wash." She bumps her hip into me playfully, but I don't budge.

"You cooked, let me help. I'll wash and you can dry." I know it's silly, but this simple act of washing the dishes has brought a sense of calm to my world. It's how I remember my parents ending meals when Dad was home and something I can envision with Kellie. Maybe even pulling up a stepstool for Rory to help wash the spoons the way my mom always let me. I haven't spent time with Kellie and Rory together, yet, but I want to. I catch myself smiling while thinking about the future and what it may hold.

"Okay, I'll agree this time, but only because you're too cute for me to refuse you anything."

I'm not sure she realizes what she said, or maybe she did. Either way, it opens a door I will gladly walk through. Everything about today has been hard, until now. I see a sliver of happiness and want to grab on to it with both hands and not let go. Forget about everything that has happened over the past week and live only in this moment.

"Oh, really?" I offer a sly grin. "You can't refuse me anything, huh?"

"You know what I mean." Kellie's blush spreads over her cheeks.

"Let's put this to the test." I rinse my hands and dry them on the towel Kellie was using earlier. "What would you say if I was to ask for a kiss?"

Kellie doesn't reply immediately. She chews on her bottom lip and appears to be weighing her options.

Waiting for her answer is torture. All I can think of is taking her in my arms, kissing and caressing her delicate skin.

My cock swells with anticipation, pressing hard against my zipper.

Finally, she puts me out of my misery. Her response is music to my ears. "I'd like that, a kiss I mean."

We promised to take things slow. I tell myself this is just a kiss and nothing more. Only I don't want just a kiss or to take it slow right now. Slow won't let me forget the events of this horrible day. Lifting her up, I slide her onto the countertop, at the perfect height to claim the kiss I want so badly. My hands hold steady on her hips. I'm afraid if I let go and allow my hands to wander over the places I crave to touch, I won't stop.

"Lance. I know today has been terrible. I've been there, remember. Tonight, lets focus on us and push aside the bad memories." She places her palms on my cheeks gently, as if I were made of glass. "Let me do this for you, Lance."

Taking control, Kellie softly presses her lips to mine. The puff of her warm breath causes goosebumps to explode on my skin.

I want to take over, crush my lips to hers, but it's not time. The sensible voice in my head shouts a reminder. *Go slow.* I'm holding on by a thread and not sure how much more I can take.

Kellie's tongue glides along the seam of my lips. She wraps her legs around my waist, pulling me into the perfect spot and grinds against my straining cock. One more circle of her hips draws out a breathy moan. "Lance, take me to bed now."

That's all it takes for my control to snap. I want to lose myself in this woman for hours. "Are you sure? We agreed to take things slow."

With a tilt of her head and a devilish grin she says, "Fuck slow."

18

KELLIE

Emerging from a deep and contented sleep, it takes a moment for me to gather my bearings. It's my bedroom, but nothing about waking up next to a man is familiar anymore. There has only been a couple of guys I've stayed overnight with, but it was before Rory came to live with me, and they never stepped foot inside this house.

My head rests on Lance's bare chest. His smooth skin feels good beneath my fingertips. The tanned muscled man I'm currently using as a pillow snores sweetly but never one to lay in bed after my eyes open, I try to extricate myself from the protective cocoon Lance has me wrapped up in without waking him. Moving at a snail's pace, my attempt to get up is thwarted as his muscles flex and he holds me still. Sneaky man isn't asleep after all.

"Good Morning, beautiful." Lance kisses the top of my head.

"Good Morning, Sir Lancelot."

"Oh, God," he groans, but seems good natured about my little joke. "I should have never told you my secret."

"Nope, you probably shouldn't have. But you did and now I get to use it when ever I want."

"You think so, huh?" In an unexpected move, Lance flips me onto my back and straddles my hips. With a wicked smile, he wiggles his fingers as if he's ready to tickle me the way he did last night. My muscles involuntarily tense, anticipating his next move.

Instead of tickling me, Lance uses his fingers to tease with featherlight strokes over my shoulders, down my arms and back up again. He massages the muscles in my shoulders and neck.

"That feels good. Don't stop." My voice is breathy and full of need.

"Turn over and I'll rub your back."

Lying on my stomach, Lance continues working on my muscles. "You're very good at this." Relaxing under his touch, I sigh with contentment.

"Now, what was it you said earlier?" Lance's hand's have settled on my hips, only his thumbs rubbing small circles.

"I have no idea what you mean."

"Allow me to refresh your memory." With that he takes me by surprise and tickles me relentlessly. "I think it was something about calling me Lancelot whenever you wanted to."

"Okay, I give. I won't call you Lancelot ever again. Stop... tickling...me." Out of breath, I beg, but not really wanting him to stop either.

"Alright, I'll show mercy this time." Lance's eyes seem brighter than yesterday. Hearing his laughter mixed with mine, my heart fills with delight. After everything Lance has been through, I'd let him tickle me for hours if it made him smile.

"You are my knight in shining armor, Sir..." I pause, waiting for Lance's reaction.

He cocks an eyebrow, daring me to finish my sentence.

"Uh, Sir Lance," I quickly add, "I wasn't going to call you Lancelot, I swear. Scout's honor." I hold up two fingers the way I think a boy scout does when pledging an oath to be trustworthy and honorable.

"Smartass." With a smile that meets his eyes, Lance adjusts my fingers into the correct position. "First of all, it's three fingers. Second, I'm sure you weren't a boy scout, Kellie, so you don't get to use that pledge of trust."

"How would you know? Were you a boy scout?"

"As a matter of fact, I was. From Tiger Cub to Eagle Scout."

"I stand corrected." An image pops to mind of a young Lance standing with a yellow bandana around his neck. "I bet you looked adorable with all those achievement patches stitched onto your uniform."

"Yeah, adorable. I'd prefer those pictures my mom has hanging in her house were burned, but she loves them. It was something for Dad and me to do together so I stuck with it longer than a lot of my friends. Making Eagle Scout was important to Dad since he got his when he was eighteen."

"You really did follow in your father's footsteps. Did you like being in scouts?"

"Not always, but the chance to hang out with my dad made it worth it."

Lance sits quiet as if in thought. By the somber expression on his face, it's not happy times occupying his mind.

"Well, Lance." I draw out his name slowly, hoping my teasing will shift the conversation back to fun and playful. "I'm starving. Can I make you a breakfast fit for a king?" I stifle a giggle.

Lance stands beside the bed and shakes his head at my corny joke. "If I'm the king, then you must be my queen." He bows slightly, reaching out I assume to help me out of bed. When I accept, he brings my hand to his lips, placing sweet kisses over each knuckle.

My heart beats double time. *He really is my knight in shining armor.*

I finish detangling myself from the sheets, open my dresser drawer, find an oversized T-shirt and yoga pants to wear. It's early Saturday morning and I have no plans to leave the house so comfort is a must.

Lance unzips a mysterious black duffle bag. He removes jeans and a dark grey T-shirt for himself. Minus underwear, he pulls on the pants, leaving them unsnapped then tugs on his shirt. I'm totally on board with his choice to go commando but I'm slightly disappointed when he covers his muscular chest and eye-catching abs.

"Where did those clothes come from." I'm baffled.

"I always carry a go bag with spare clothes in my truck. Something to change into in case of an emergency. Once certain I wouldn't wake you, I hurried outside, grabbed my bag, and climbed back into bed hoping you wouldn't notice I was gone."

"I'm surprised I didn't wake up. I'm usually a light sleeper and hear every peep Rory makes."

Stepping up behind me, Lance's arms pull me back toward his body. He rests his chin on my shoulder and whispers, "Well, we did have quite the workout last night."

My muscles turn to jelly as his warm breath on my neck has my body aching for more. Tilting my head to the side, I give Lance access to that special place I love to have kissed. The scratch of his beard on my skin brings on a wave of goosebumps, almost buckling my knees with desire. Turning in his arms, I look up into his eyes, silently begging for Lance to grant me more passionate kisses, just like the ones we shared last night.

Without urgency, our lips touch. As the heat builds between us, my need for more takes hold. Greedily, I part my lips and deepen the kiss. A tangling of tongues, gliding and teasing each other. The intensity of our kiss slows to a more tender and sweeter pace. Placing the palms of my hands onto Lance's chest, I feel a rapid heartbeat that matches my own.

We both struggle to slow our breathing. Although staying in Lance's arms all day sounds fantastic, it's not realistic or smart. I tell myself the raw passion from last night still running through my veins will have to keep me satisfied for now. It's important we learn more about each other before falling into bed again.

Somehow finding the strength to step away from the man I've come to crave, I break the intimate moment for our own good. "Come on, big guy. Waffles, sausage, and eggs are on the menu. You can make the coffee."

Like a coward, I escape to the kitchen quickly before Lance can respond. It would only take a simple glance from him to change my plans from eating breakfast to dragging him back to my bed and never letting him go.

After breakfast, Lance and I sit on the front porch swing talking as we finish our coffee. It's a special moment sharing stories from our childhood. It seems Lance was quite the troublemaker behind that Eagle Scout exterior. Nothing major, but a lot more exciting than my boring life.

He was caught cheating on a test in fourth grade, a few silly little pranks in high school, and one big drunken party in college where his father was on duty and ironically was called out on a noise complaint.

"Imagine standing shoulder to shoulder with your buddies, as if we were a bunch of new recruits. My father walked up and down the line, lecturing us about drinking and causing a ruckus in the neighborhood. We were all of legal drinking age, but he didn't care." Lance pushes off, putting the swing into motion.

"I never did much drinking in college. My sister's antics cured me of the desire to overindulge. I've rarely felt more than a buzz."

"It was the last party I attended. Nobody wanted the cop's son there just in case my dad showed up again. I was humiliated at the time, but looking back, and with the things I've seen since becoming a cop, I understand what he was saying. His biggest concern was that we hadn't set up sober rides."

"I can respect your father wanting to keep everyone safe." I take a sip of coffee. "After watching Leslie drive while high on God knows what, I make a point of never driving if I've had even one drink. Thankfully, I didn't have to worry about her driving with Rory, since she didn't have a car. It was only the other things I had to deal with."

"You know I remember that day clearly. I figured it was just another call about someone who'd overdosed in that shithole apartment complex. We were there almost every day that week for one reason or another." Lance rests his arm behind me on the back of the swing.

"I try not to think about it too much, but I can't forget it entirely either. When I do think of it though, you're always part of the memory." I snuggle into his side. "I've carried the handkerchief you gave me as a reminder of you and how kind you were to us."

"I saw you with it at the funeral and wondered why you still had it."

"Somehow I knew you and I had a bigger connection. You've been the man locked in my thoughts for months." Was I revealing too much, too soon? "I was shocked to run into you at Heath's. I figured you were going to live in my dreams, never my reality." Maybe I should be embarrassed for admitting I've fantasized about Lance as the man I want to spend the rest of my life with; the one Rory could look at as the father she never had, but we've already moved at warp speed. I may as well lay it all out there now.

"Is that what you meant by you've been mine for a long time?"

I look into his eyes and gage his reaction. "Yes. You probably think I'm crazy, don't you?"

"Not at all. I told Paul about you and how I wished we'd have met some other way. I was drawn to you, too. So no, I don't think you're crazy at all."

"My friends didn't understand my obsession over a man I knew nothing about. I told myself, if I was ever lucky enough to find you, I'd take a chance on getting to know the man behind the badge."

"So, tell me, when you think of me, what springs to mind?"

Climbing onto Lance's lap, I straddle him with complete confidence and tell him exactly who Deputy Lancelot Malloy is to me. "You're mine."

Convincing Lance to return for dinner tonight took little effort. A few kisses, the promise of a homecooked meal, and he was putty in my hands. His only request was something sweet for dessert.

Making a list of things I'll need from the grocery store I catch myself drawing hearts while thinking of last night. It was more than sex, at least for me. I want so much more than a bed partner and honestly believe Lance is that person. Perhaps I'm getting ahead of myself, but I can see a real future with Lance.

Closing my eyes, I picture Lance and me walking in the park with Rory. She's holding our hands, swinging between us just like I've seen other families do. Our smiles are bright and full of joy. I think about re-introducing Rory to Lance so he can see how much she's grown.

With my grocery list finished and covered in hearts, I decide to Facetime Rory. It was too late for me to talk with her last night like I normally would do on an overnight at my parents.

I prop my phone up against the vase on my dining table and wait for them to answer. When Rory's face appears on my screen it hits me how much I miss having her with me.

"Addy K, Grumpa is snoring. Wanna see?"

She doesn't know how to switch the camera lens around, so she turns the whole phone. I can see my dad sound asleep in his recliner. I listen carefully, yep, he's snoring like a buzz saw.

"Rory, let Grumpa sleep. I want to see you, turn the phone around, please."

Seeing her smiling face again, I ask, "Where's Gram Gram?" I know she's not too far away since she had to answer the call before passing the phone to Rory.

"Kitchen. Wanna see?" The bouncing image tells me she's already walking in that direction.

"Gram Gram, Addy K wants you."

"Hi, Kellie. We missed your call last night. Is everything okay?"

"Yeah, Mom, just an emotional day with the funeral. I went to bed early." It's not a lie since Lance and I were in bed before the sun went down.

"Of course, dear. Funerals are hard on our hearts and minds. Are you still planning on eating Sunday dinner here tomorrow night?"

"Sure, I'll bring the dessert. What are you making?" I figure if I'm making a cake for Lance, I can easily make two.

"Smothered pork chops, rice and a green salad fresh from the garden. Rory and I have been outside all morning, pulling weeds and sprucing up the area around the veggies. Isn't that right Rory?"

Somewhere in the distance I hear Rory shout, "Right, Gram Gram."

"She's too busy building puzzles to be bothered with us.

She's been an angel and a great helper." Mom's love for her granddaughter shines through when she talks about Rory.

"Sure. She's an angel with you. I get the barf and sleepless nights." I chuckle because it's true, but I wouldn't change a thing.

"Welcome to parenthood. You take the good with the bad, but every minute is worth it."

"I know, I'm just teasing. You know how much I love my little girl. I miss her a ton already. I'll show up early tomorrow and help make dinner." I wonder if it's too soon to ask Lance to come to meet my parents for Sunday dinner. I add it to the growing list of things I want to talk with him about tonight.

"Sounds good. Rory, come say bye to Addy K."

Mom uses the touch screen to flip the camera around and I see Rory at her little table covered in puzzles. Without looking up, she calls out to me. "Bye, Addy K. Love you lots."

"Love you more, baby. I'll see you tomorrow for dinner. Bye Mom, love you, and Dad too."

"Love you more, Kellie. See you tomorrow night." Mom repeats the words I use for Rory. Who do you think I learned it from?

With my grocery list in hand, I grab an arm load of reusable bags and almost jog to my car. To say I'm anxious for Lance to return is an understatement. I turn on the radio while driving and sing along to a romantic song by George Strait, *I Cross My Heart*.

Why do love songs always sound better when you're actually in love? Wait? Love? Do I love Lance?

My heart begins to flutter as I realize, yes, I am in love with Deputy Lance Malloy.

19

LANCE

A warm breeze blows through my truck windows as I sing along to an old eighties classic playing on the radio, reminding me of the days when life was less complicated. Although I'm not sure if my world can be any more mixed up than it is right now.

How I wish I could go back in time and retain every vital piece of knowledge I know now. But that's just a pipedream since life doesn't work that way. The universe has a way of throwing the good and bad at us when we least expect it.

One issue forces its way to the forefront of my mind, and I can't decide whether spending the night in Kellie's bed was the right or wrong thing at this stage. I don't regret anything because I feel as if we've known each other for much longer than a week. But my world is a strange place right now. A week feels like a lifetime, bogged down in an endless roller-coaster of emotions.

Spending time with Kellie allows me a small glimpse of hope and there's a part of me that feels I can finally veer off the shitty direction my life has unexpectedly taken and turn toward something good.

Still, I'm torn how to proceed.

Do I jump in with both feet or remain cautious?

It's a decision I must make because I don't want the loss of Paul to sway any decision that will affect my future. I want to be with Kellie because of who she is and what she means to me, not because she fills a gap left by Paul.

Tonight, I plan to tell her what I think and how I feel. Hopefully, we are on the same page but until we both lay our cards on the table, there is no chance of moving forward. Falling in love and potentially stepping into the role of step-parent wasn't something I saw coming. In fact, I'm blind-sided, but blame the universe again; taking somebody I love away from me and sending someone else to fill the void is part of the grand scheme of things. I can seek all the answers I like, but they will never come.

My doubt is offset by something my mother used to say to me and today in particular her words have come back to slap me across the cheek. I repeat her words out loud. "When life runs smooth, it's meant to be. However, when life is full of obstacles and fighting to make something work, you're on the wrong path and it's time to change direction." Right now, I don't see anything blocking our road to happiness, but my own indecision.

I'm home before I know it.

Locking my truck, I feel lighter as I walk into my house. When leaving yesterday, all I felt was unspeakable dread and a cloud of misery looming over my home. Today, I see sunshine casting a bright light of hope across every shadow it touches.

I drop the pile of mail onto the kitchen table, planning to rummage through it later. I should open it now, but all I want is a long, hot, relaxing shower, and to change into something that hasn't been sitting in my go bag for months.

Stripping out of my clothes, I toss them into the hamper and place my wallet on the dresser. When I search for my phone in the pocket of my discarded jeans, I realize I never turned it back on after the funeral. I power it up while walking to the shower.

My phone pings to tell me I have messages. Staring at the screen, several are from Jackson.

Jackson: *Hey Lance. Have you been home yet?*

Jackson: *Since you're not replying to me, I'll assume you're still with Kellie. Call me when you get a chance.*

Jackson: *Dude, call me.*

Shit, I bet he's worried about me. I should have checked in with him after the funeral and decided to call him right away.

He answers after two rings. "Lance. Hey man, everything good with you?"

"Yeah! I'm sorry I didn't call you back earlier. You were right, I was with Kellie."

"It's cool. I just want to check if there is anything you need."

"I'm good, but thanks."

"Anytime."

His concern means a lot to me. "You know, I got to thinking, and I'm sure Paul would hate me feeling sorry for myself."

"He would, you're right."

"I need to move on and find a way to live without him."

Jackson exhales loudly. "Lance. Don't try to rush yourself through the grieving process."

"I'm not." He was right as usual, I was doing exactly that.

"Grief doesn't have a timeline or a script for that matter."

"I'm doing the best I can, Jackson."

"At some point you'll need to deal with Paul's passing and I'm here when that time comes."

"I'm already dealing with it."

"No, you're not. You're rushing into something because it keeps your mind off what it should be trying to process."

I hate the fact he knows me too well, but his words hit home.

Maybe I am going at breakneck speed with Kellie because she is a distraction. That isn't fair to her or me. "I'm walking a thin line here, man, and trying not to fall."

"You're gonna fall, Lance, whether you want to or not and yeah, you might delay the inevitable but it'll happen and the sooner you realize that and let it be, the better you'll feel in the long run."

"I can't lose myself in this."

"This what, Lance?"

"Grief."

"Then what is the alternative? To lose yourself in the bed of that gorgeous girl of yours?"

"It's not like that."

"Isn't it?"

"No," I snapped, anger rising quickly. "I wouldn't use Kellie."

"I wasn't suggesting you were but think about it for a minute." He took a breath. "Your partner and best friend takes his own life and immediately you occupy your time with that sweet girl you first met while dealing with her drugged-up sister."

"It's fate."

"Maybe, but fate has shitty timing, Lance, you gotta see that."

I could see exactly what he was saying. Fate took Paul away from me and replaced him with Kellie. I had not had time to sit and fully process my life in this last week. Paul is dead and will never come back but Kellie is here and ready to commit, I can feel it. But now isn't the time to make such a momentous decision, no matter how much I want it too. "What am I gonna do, I really like her?"

"Take some time and think carefully." He pauses, allowing me to absorb his words. "That's all I ask because when you fall you could take Kellie and her little girl down with you, and I know you well enough to know you don't want that for them."

I didn't want to have this conversation right now. "If I need anything, Jackson, I know who to call." But to ease Jackson's worry, I tried to put a positive spin on the situation. "This thing with Kellie is better than I ever could have expected. I'm going back to her house for dinner tonight."

"Sounds good man, and I'm not trying to ruin things. I can see how good a match you are for one another. I only want you to think before you make any big decisions."

"I hear what you're saying, and promise I won't rush in."

"Okay, but I'm here when you're ready to talk."

"Thanks, man." Having him on my side was a stroke of luck. "I need to go…"

"Before you do, a few of the guys want to meet at Heath's for lunch tomorrow around noon. We need to schedule the Sheriff's annual fun run for the Special Olympics."

In the past, Paul would dress up like a clown and make balloon animals for the kids, but he won't be there this time. Reality smacks me in the face and my chest begins to tighten at the thought of never working beside my partner ever again. My temples begin to throb with the onset of a headache. I guess the rollercoaster ride isn't ready to slow down quite yet. Without him, I feel no enthusiasm for an event I used to love.

"Lance, you can bring Kellie if it makes it easier for you."

"Are you sure?"

"Of course. We need all the help we can get, so no excuses; I expect to see you there tomorrow."

"I'm not promising anything, but I'll talk to Kellie." I feel anxious, every doubt within me scrambling to the surface. "If she's available, we'll be there." I wasn't sure I would ask her, or even mention it because I had no idea if I would go myself. "Now, I need to get ready for my date so talk to ya later."

"See you tomorrow," he replies. "It'll be a good day."

"Okay, looking forward to it." I lie to him because in that split second, I decide I'm not going. I can't sit with co-workers who will only remind me about the things I'm trying to forget.

I feel relaxed after my shower and focus my thoughts back to Kellie. Dinner is still several hours away, and my appetite has finally returned. I make two ham sandwiches, add a handful of *Doritos* to my plate and pop the top on a bottle of *Blue Moon*. Sitting at the dining table, I sort through the pile of mail. Water bill, several pieces of junk mail, and a large padded envelope with my name and address written in blue ink.

I tuck a few chips between the slices of bread and take a big crunchy bite. It reminds me of the way I ate sandwiches as a kid.

Curious what could be inside the big envelope, I open it first, shaking the contents onto the table. I freeze the moment I see a picture of Paul and me at our graduation ceremony, proudly wearing our new badges.

No longer hungry, I slide my plate to the center of the table and sort through everything in front of me. Another envelope, more pictures, a Springhill Sheriff's Department patch and a brass name tag; Deputy P. Lancaster.

I push myself away from the table and pace the floor,

trying to rein in the whirlwind of emotions running through my body. *What the fuck is this and who sent it?* I look at the address on the front of the envelope again and recognize Paul's messy handwriting. Cold sweat runs down my back. I tremble from head to toe when full realization hits me. This could be the last communication from my partner.

Picking up the pictures, I study each one carefully. They are all of Paul and me from the past eight years. One of us covered in mud from the obstacle course, another picture I remember Jane taking of us holding up the trophy from a darts tournament, and several more from their wedding.

Downing the rest of my beer, I walk to the fridge for another but change my mind. This shit calls for something much stronger. I grab a tall glass and fill it with ice. Reaching into the back of the liquor cabinet, I find what I'm searching for, an unopened bottle of *Jack Daniel's No. 27 Gold*. Paul bought it years ago, promising to drink it with me when we had a good enough reason to open it. If this package is what I think it is, it's the closest Paul and I will ever come to sharing it.

Cracking the seal on the bottle, I pour a small amount into the glass. Just enough for me to taste and maybe provide the liquid courage I'll need to move on to the next envelope. Closing my eyes, I bring the glass to my lips, pausing to smell the rich oak and smokey aroma from the aged whiskey. I swallow the liquid, enjoying the slow burn running down my throat. I have no doubt, Paul would have loved this. I pour more over the ice.

Quit stalling. You know what it is, now open it.

I take another sip, then hesitate on drinking anymore. I need to be sober while reading this letter and push the bottle away. I walk over to sit on the couch, take a deep breath, and open the smaller envelope.

My breathing hitches as I read the first word.

I can hear Paul's voice in my mind.

. . .

Hey buddy,

Forgive me for doing it this way but I couldn't leave without giving you some answers.

I bet you're angry and think you failed me somehow. I promise you, you didn't, and I hope this letter can provide you with some comfort by telling you why I made my choice. Months ago, I made the decision to die, realizing no life is better than the half-life I've been trying to live. It was always going to happen, but I had to get my shit in order first.

I want you to understand because if it wasn't for you, I wouldn't have lasted as long as I did.

Every day, I pretended things were perfect, but you knew the truth. You saw the struggle behind my smile and tried to get me help, but I wouldn't listen.

As weird as it sounds, I needed to hang on to the pain. In my mind, the hurt I felt was Jane reminding me to not forget her. But living in pain, wanting someone you'll never see again is merely existing.

It wasn't just losing Jane that pushed me to make the decision to end my life. Other things played a part too.

There was a time when I was proud to be a Deputy in the Springhill Sheriff's Department. Helping others has always been in my blood, but after years of witnessing hatred, violent attacks, abuse, and death, I can't do it anymore.

I know there will be those who won't understand why and will judge me. But no matter what they think, I will rest happily knowing I will be with Jane for eternity.

You're the best friend any man could ever have. Don't feel sorry for me. This is what I want. I'll be dancing in the stars with Jane forever more.

. . .

I read the letter three times trying to absorb his words. Each time, I sense darkness creep in, surrounding me. Jane's death was an obvious factor, but I had no idea the job he once loved was destroying him as well.

My breathing intensifies and white dots affect my field of vision. I'm dizzy and on the verge of passing out. I lean forward, placing my head between my knees while I attempt to control my breathing.

I thought knowing why he killed himself would help but I was wrong. It doesn't matter why now, only that he's gone. Reading Paul's final words has provided me no comfort, only breaking through the dam I built to keep my head and heart safe. Now the floodgates are wide open, and I am forced to deal with grief just as Jackson predicted.

Stuffing everything back into the large envelope, I grab my truck keys and run out the door. There's only one place I can think of where I won't be bothered, and no one will look for me.

Driving up the hillside, my truck bounces roughly over the rugged dirt trail. This road is only used for checking fires and managing controlled burns. Reaching the peak of the mountain, I cut the engine off and kill the headlights.

My breathing and the chirping of crickets are the only sound that can be heard. Switching on the dome light in the cab, I find Paul's envelope. Reaching in, I remove the patch, running my fingertips over the stitched letters spelling out the word Deputy.

Next, I remove the name tag. The one Paul pinned to his chest opposite his badge. I notice the smudges on the metal. Paul never liked polishing his brass or boots, only doing it on inspection day. He'd say, "I can do my job just as well, with or without shiny boots or sparkling metal pinned to my uniform."

I take the picture of us from graduation and prop it up in front of me, covering the speedometer. We were rookies ready to take on the world. Fresh, untainted to the realities of what being in law enforcement really means. Paul loved being a cop. When did that change?

Thankfully, I'd forgotten to take my go bag into the house earlier. I unzip it and unpin my badge from the dress shirt folded inside.

Resting my wrists on top of the steering wheel, I hold my badge in front of me and inspect it closely. Number 1659, one digit from Paul's. New doubts overshadow the ones from earlier. Is the stress that comes with this job worth it? What if I reach my breaking point, where would that leave Kellie and Rory? What if I'm already broken? Maybe they'd be better off without me?

Panic engulfs me as I make the hardest decision of my life. I can't be with Kellie, nor give her what she needs. Until I come to grips with my own emotions, I'll never be the man she deserves.

Starting the engine, I slam the truck into gear and drive down the mountain faster than I should, kicking up a cloud of dust behind me. I have no idea where I'm going, but I know if I don't get out of here now, I'm in danger of never finding my way back.

I think of Kellie, sitting, waiting for me to knock at the door. Stomping on my brakes, I skid to a stop. I can't leave without contacting her. She deserves an explanation, but what do I say that will make any of what I'm doing right? Tears sting my eyes because my actions are going to hurt her.

I pick up my phone and scroll to her number. I'm not brave enough to hear her voice because I know for all the wrong reasons I'll stay when I need to go.

My finger hovers over the send button, but I hit it anyway.

Me: I'm so sorry, Kellie.

. . .

I don't have to wait long for her reply.

Kellie: What for?

Me: I'm leaving, and I don't know when or if I'm coming back. Please forgive me.

I press send and immediately turn off my phone, knowing she will call. It's the act of a coward, but I can't deal with her heartbreak on top of my grief.

My head says this is for the best for everyone.

My heart says I just threw away my only chance at true love.

"Forgive me," I whisper, before dropping my phone onto the passenger seat and speeding off into the unknown.

To be continued in Forever Blue, Book 2

ALSO BY KAYLEE ROSE

Thank you for reading the first book of Lance and Kellie's story. The trilogy continues with Forever Blue! Get the entire trilogy now!

The Weight Of The Badge Trilogy

For the Love of Us: Fighting to Keep Our Love Alive

ROMAN: Hot In the City - The Whole Story
Co-written with Zane Michaelson

Don't miss my latest series Vegas Venom Baseball!

Payoff Pitch Book 1 – Micha Powell
Owning the Game Book 2 - Dylan Brooks
Strike Three Book 3 - Chris Tucker
Game Changer Book 4 - RJ Cannon

LAW ENFORCEMENT RESOURCES

Resources for officers and their family members who may be struggling.

CopLine offers a confidential 24-hour hotline answered by retired law enforcement officers who have gone through a strenuous vetting and training process to become an active listener.
Hotline: 1-800-COPLINE (267-5463)

Safe Call Now is a confidential, comprehensive, 24-hour crisis referral service for all public safety employees, all emergency services personnel, and their family members nationwide.
SAFE CALL NOW: 1-206-459-3020

Under the Shield
(855) 889-2348

NATIONAL SUICIDE PREVENTION LIFELINE
1-800-273-TALK (8255)

CHECK OUT VEGAS VENOM BASEBALL!

Vegas Venom Baseball Romance Series.
Venom Baseball romance novels are stand-alone books that
are best read in order.
Each couple will reappear throughout future stories as the
wide, wide world of Vegas Venom Baseball grows.

Payoff Pitch Book 1
Whoever said out of sight, out of mind must be crazy.
There wasn't a day since I left that I didn't think about her.
As much as I wanted to stay with her in Boulder City, it was
never an option.
Caroline had big dreams of becoming a chef, and I'd just
signed my rookie contract.
It was the chance of a lifetime for both of us.
After years of no contact, I'd assumed I'd lost her for good,
but when I injured my pitching arm, I was given a second
chance to right the wrongs from the past.
This is my last chance and the biggest payoff pitch of my life.

ACKNOWLEDGMENTS

To my husband and sons, without your love and support, I would never have had the courage to become a published author. You always believe I can do anything I put my heart into, even when I can't see it myself. I love you more.

To the law enforcement officers throughout the world and their families, Thank you for all you do.

Gloria, Thank you for your friendship and for being the other half of Double Trouble Book Club. You are the organized brain, I'm the silly entertainment and somehow it just works.

Carol, your help while navigating through the book world is invaluable. I will never be able to thank you enough for all you do.

Zane Michaelson, Thank you for your continued support and always reminding me everyone starts somewhere.

Maggie Jane Schuler, Thank you for guiding and encouraging me from the beginning.

Michelle Cooper and Sue Johns, Thank you for your support and always believing in me.

To my editor Mina, I am forever grateful for your patience while I navigate my way through the world of self-publishing.

THANK YOU
~Kaylee Rose
xoxo

ABOUT THE AUTHOR

Kaylee Rose is a wife, mother, sports fan, and contemporary romance author looking to stretch her creative muscles and explore other genres as well.

Inspired by her husband's career in law enforcement, and her passion for the written word, Kaylee began to pen her novels as an escape from the rigors of everyday life.

Kaylee's series, The Weight of the Badge, was written after attending law enforcement classes with her husband. The seminars focused on the stress a first responder faces daily, how it affects their lives both on and off the job and the continually growing number of law enforcement suicides. With her books and her experience married to a law enforcement officer, Kaylee found herself armed with the perfect platform to use her voice and subtly spread the statistics others may not know. Kaylee Rose is passionate about sharing sexy stories with an important message mixed in.

Kaylee's husband is her biggest supporter, believing in her even when she can not, and writing love stories comes naturally to her after falling in love with him at first sight.

FROM KAYLEE ROSE
AND ZANE MICHAELSON

ROMAN: Hot In the City - The Whole Story

For Roman, sexual gratification is the ultimate high; addictive and all-consuming. It must be attained, no matter the cost to himself or the Blackthorne family reputation.

Considered by many to be handsome, arrogant, and tough, within him sits a ruthless determination to succeed, no matter who he steps on to achieve his goals.

But at the forefront of his actions lies the need for praise, and what better way to stroke his out-of-control ego than to seduce the lonely, bored housewives of upper-crust society and occasionally their willing daughters, or sons, amongst others.

Not averse to broadening his horizons, Roman plays the field while refusing to use gender as a barrier to halt winning the ultimate prize; the hedonistic pursuit of pleasure and sensual self-indulgence.

But with that craving for more, and his wilful refusal to look past his own desires, danger creeps out of the shadows intent on punishing Roman for past mistakes.

Designed to melt your Kindle, this is the combined 'Hot In the City' series by best-selling authors, Zane Michaelson, and Kaylee Rose...enjoy the ride because it's a wild one!

Ebook * Paperback

Made in the USA
Middletown, DE
23 September 2023

39144728R00125